W9-BVQ-021

"I owe you an apology, Blake Connors!"

Karin's voice was serious. It had become quite apparent to her this evening—that quality he had of genuine concern, generosity and goodwill toward others. A lump rose in her throat, and trying to lighten the moment, she gave a gurgle of laughter. "I had you pegged right the first time. Santa Claus!"

He grinned sheepishly. "Now you're pulling my leg. Just this afternoon you accused me of—"

"I was wrong!" She couldn't seem to stop laughing. She felt happy and in a very festive mood as she pointed a finger at him. "Definitely Santa Claus. And with you, it's always Christmas!"

"And with you, Karin Palmer, everything's unpredictable! One minute you're a spitfire, and the next..." He shrugged. "But never mind about that. *This* is the mood I love."

Eva Rutland began writing when her four children, now all successful professionals, were growing up. She has become a regular—and very popular—contributor to Harlequin's Romance and Regency series. Eva lives in California with her husband, Bill, who actively supports and encourages her writing career.

Books by Eva Rutland

HARLEQUIN ROMANCE
2897—TO LOVE THEM ALL
2944—AT FIRST SIGHT
3064—NO ACCOUNTING FOR LOVE

HARLEQUIN REGENCY ROMANCE
 1—MATCHED PAIR
20—THE VICAR'S DAUGHTER
28—ENTERPRISING LADY
45—THE WILLFUL LADY

ALWAYS CHRISTMAS
Eva Rutland

Harlequin Books

TORONTO • NEW YORK • LONDON
AMSTERDAM • PARIS • SYDNEY • HAMBURG
STOCKHOLM • ATHENS • TOKYO • MILAN
MADRID • WARSAW • BUDAPEST • AUCKLAND

ISBN 0-373-03240-4

Harlequin Romance first edition December 1992

ALWAYS CHRISTMAS

CHAPTER ONE

KARIN SAT on the bar stool and absently tapped her fingers on the counter. She'd allowed herself one year to get the business on a firm footing; that left almost seven months. By Christmas, she'd told her aunt, she should be rolling in money.

But now... Would she have to give it all up before summer had hardly begun?

She sat up straight. All right. The breakdown of her bus that morning was unfortunate. But people in business ought to be prepared for emergencies. She'd manage somehow.

Karin sat at the bar near the back entrance of Harrah's Lake Tahoe casino, trying to work things out. She was oblivious to the continuous and not-too-distant racket of slot machines, the clanking of falling coins and the occasional jackpot bell announcing a lucky winner. The loan of Mr. Turner's old bus was the main reason she'd been able to start her business on a shoestring. But this morning the old engine had conked out just as they reached the halfway point. "Burned out," Bert, her driver, had said. She'd have to replace it. And Bert said that would cost—

She frowned as her eyes focused on a drink that had been set before her. She stared at it, wondering. She hadn't ordered anything.

"Scotch and soda." A man's nasal twang cut through the casino's background noise. "Don't you like it?"

She shook her head, not looking at him. She was still wrestling with the problem that had plagued her for the past six hours. She hadn't panicked this morning, or at least it hadn't shown. She had remained cool and professional. She'd had that nice patrolman phone for a replacement bus and when it came she'd continued with her passengers to the casino, leaving Bert to wait for the tow truck. But while the ladies enjoyed themselves, Karin had spent the whole day juggling figures in her mind. She should have been better prepared for emergencies. But this was more than an emergency; it was a catastrophe. She sighed. Okay, she reminded herself, the bank balance showed two thousand, six hundred fifty-four dollars and fifteen cents. If she—

"Oh. So what's your preference? Screwdriver? Tom Collins? Anything you like."

"Thank you. I mean, no thank you. Nothing," she said, giving him a brief glance. He was rather paunchy and breathed heavily as he slid onto the bar stool beside her.

"Having any luck?" he asked.

"No." Karin turned away, but she smiled, remembering one of Uncle Bob's sayings when things went wrong—"If it wasn't for bad luck, I wouldn't have any luck at all."

"I had a great run of luck at the blackjack table just now." The man took a long swallow of his drink. "But then I started on keno and I swear... You see, I use this system..." He went on to detail his method of play.

Karin wished he would leave. *She* couldn't. She'd told the driver of the replacement bus to meet her here, where it was relatively quiet and she could keep an eye on her group.

"Do you come up here often?" asked the man.

She shook her head.

"I try to make it at least once a week, usually on Mondays. See, I figure the weekend crowds leave the machines loaded and so..."

The man rambled on some more and Karin nodded vaguely, trying to block out his voice as she returned to her calculations. According to Bert, it would cost no less than five thousand to replace the burned-out engine. Add to this the cost of the replacement bus and the tow truck. The figures danced through her head as she added, subtracted and came to the conclusion that she would need—

The man leaned closer. "Do you mind if I ask are you married?"

For the first time she looked at him directly, with what she hoped was a squelching frown. "Do you mind if I ask are you rich?"

It worked. He sidled away, muttering, "Just trying to be friendly."

"I am." The voice on her left was deep, decisive and unmistakably suggestive.

Another creep! Karin wheeled around. She didn't have time for this. But the man's twinkling eyes and genial smile told her he was teasing. She took a deep breath and grinned back. Unable to resist, she joined in the joke.

"How rich *are* you?" she asked.

"How rich do I have to be?" he countered.

"Three thousand, three hundred forty-five dollars and eighty-five cents," she said promptly, then was appalled at herself. It had just popped out. The exact amount she'd calculated.

His grin widened. "Oh. I see. Only moderately rich. And you're very precise about the amount. Might I ask how you arrived at that figure?"

"Painfully," she answered, warming to what appeared to be genuine interest. "After repeated—"

"All set. Are you ready?" It was Jake Travers, the driver of the replacement bus. Karin was ridiculously glad to see him. She had been on the verge of revealing her private concerns to a perfect stranger!

"Just about," she said, jumping down from the stool. "Give me a few minutes to round up my people."

"Take all the time you need," Jake said, settling himself on the stool she had just vacated and ordering, "A tall, tall glass of ginger ale."

The noise became almost deafening as she moved into the midst of the arena. The ringing bells, the constant pinging of coins, the clanking of the machines, all assaulted her ears as she threaded her way among the gamblers to single out the women who'd come with her. It took some time to gather up everyone.

"I've had such marvelous luck!" squealed little Mrs. Jackson. "Dear me, is it time to leave already? Oh, Karin, honey, would you take this to the cashier for me?"

After she had cashed out Mrs. Jackson's three buckets of nickles, she helped Mrs. Conway, who used a walker, to the ladies' room. Several others also availed themselves of this opportunity, although she told them there was a lavatory on the bus, a convenience not available on her own twenty-five-passenger coach. Then she had to find Mrs. Leslie's sweater. "I think I left it over there on that chair where I was playing keno," the elderly woman told her, frowning. "But now I don't see it..."

Karin knew that with any other tour, the passengers would have had to wait outside, ready to board as soon as their vehicle arrived. But she also knew that the special service she offered was the reason she'd been engaged to convey the members of the Senior Citizen Garden Club on their trek to the casino every second Tuesday. The casinos were not her usual runs. She made this trip as a special favor to Aunt Meg's friend Laurie Jackson. "Traveling with you is like being with my own daughter," Mrs. Jackson had declared after a couple of Karin's art tours. "I feel so cared for. Now my garden club..."

And they certainly had been good sports about all the trouble today, Karin thought, as she finally led them all out. Then she went back to the entrance to beckon across the room to Jake, still sitting beside the man who had joked with her.

The stranger nodded goodbye and smiled, a smile so warm and intimate that she felt her pulses race.

"Coming?"

"Huh? Oh, yes." She turned and followed Jake out, thoroughly ashamed of herself. Gaping like a schoolgirl just because a man had a sexy smile. So intrigued by a handsome face that she'd forgotten everything else—passengers, problems, schedules. For a moment it had been just the stranger and herself.

She shook her head as she boarded the bus. This was no time to blank out problems. Where was she going to get practically four thousand dollars to replace that engine? She *had* to replace it. During the past four months, since starting her tour business, she'd certainly used the bus more than Mr. Turner had. He hardly ever used it for his choir anymore—and never on any of these steep mountain roads—the kind that burned out old engines. And he'd been so generous. She had planned to give him a big bonus when the business got off the ground, but now . . .

Would she even be able to get credit? Anyway, maybe, just maybe, Bert was wrong and things weren't so bad. *You wish!* Bert was one of the best mechanics in town.

Well, I'll deal with it when I know exactly what I'm dealing with.

Meanwhile, first things first. She tied on the lavender hostess apron Aunt Meg had made for her, stuffed one of the big pockets with little packets of nuts, filled the other with plastic cups and deftly opened a bottle of champagne. Her smile was bright and her manner one of calm cheerfulness as she started up the aisle. She would think about Mr. Turner's bus later. And she would think not at all about a certain man she'd seen in a bar and would probably never see again.

Only she couldn't stop thinking about him. She was slightly unnerved by the way she recalled every detail— the healthy glow of his tanned skin against the open collar of his snowy-white polo shirt. How his well-cut jeans hugged lean muscular thighs.

"Oh, of course you can have a refill, Mrs. Downing." Karin balanced herself as the bus rounded a curve. Then she poured the drink and heard all about Mrs. Downing's luck at the dime slots. "Good for you!" she congratulated the white-haired woman before moving on.

He was probably one of those compulsive gamblers who hang around casinos. He had that lazy casual appearance. His hair looked as if he'd just left the shower and forgotten to comb it. Sandy hair. She didn't usually find blond men attractive. She preferred men with dark hair and dark mysterious eyes. Not like his blue eyes— open and laughing and full of mischief. As if he didn't have a care in the— "Oh, I'm sorry!" she exclaimed, mopping up the champagne she'd spilled on Mrs. Jackson's skirt.

"No harm done. Polyester, you know." The elderly lady twinkled up at her. "Lovely champagne, my dear."

"Yes," Karin agreed, resolving to keep her mind on what she was doing. She was glad she'd remembered to transfer the champagne when they'd changed buses. And, of course, the sparkling cider. Several of her passengers were teetotalers.

Maybe he worked at the casino in some capacity. He certainly looked very much at home there. If they'd had a chance to talk— Oh, forget it. None of her business, anyway.

But when the whole box of packaged nuts slipped from her hand, Karin realized she was still dreaming about the man with the sexy smile. And she had more important matters to consider, she told herself as she dropped to her knees to retrieve the nuts. She had two tours scheduled for next week and no bus!

When they reached their pickup point, the Senior Citizen Center in Carmichael, Karin apologized for the inconvenience and thanked the women for being so cooperative. "I'll make it up to you on our next trip," she promised as they got off the bus. And there *would* be another trip, she told herself. She would manage somehow.

She telephoned Bert as soon as she reached home. "Yep," he said. "Engine's conked out. But it's not as much as I thought, kid. Only four thousand forty-six dollars and thirty-nine cents. Labor and all."

Big deal! Might as well be five thousand. And there was the cost of the replacement bus, not to mention the towing.

"Well, thanks, Bert. I'll go down there tomorrow and . . ." And what? "And see about it. I'll be in touch."

She hung up the phone and returned to the kitchen table, pushing aside her half-eaten sandwich.

Darn! What was she going to do?

She sat with her elbows on the table, her chin cupped in her hands, and studied the little clock on the kitchen wall. She wished she had someone to talk with. She wished Aunt Meg and Uncle Bob weren't faraway on that cruise. No. She was glad they weren't here. They'd done enough for her.

They had taken her in when she was only ten and her parents had died, and had always treated her as their own. She'd been very happy living with them. When she was eighteen she'd enrolled in a secretarial course and then taken a job with the state Department of Water Resources in Sacramento. She had felt marvelously independent, having her own income and living in the little apartment she shared with her friend Joyce.

However, within a year she'd become bored with her job typing reams of technical data day after day. She found she missed the home where she'd lived with her uncle and aunt on the outskirts of Carmichael, a small suburb of Sacramento. She missed the sunny attic room that Uncle Bob had fashioned into a studio for Meg. Margaret Palmer was an amateur artist; she enjoyed dabbling with watercolors and some oils, and she'd even sold a few of her paintings. Inspired by Meg, Karin had also begun to dabble with paints and often accompanied her on the art tours her aunt used to arrange for the Crocker Art Gallery.

"Bored, are you?" Meg had said when Karin divulged some of these feelings one Sunday afternoon at this same kitchen table. "So, quit your job."

Karin had stared in amazement at her still-attractive and vivacious fifty-year-old aunt. Uncle Bob was right when he claimed that, "Meg's a free spirit. And she doesn't give a damn about money. She thinks it grows on trees."

"My dear aunt, there is a little matter of earning a living."

"My dear niece," Meg countered, "do you know how many people get trapped by a paycheck and spend their whole lives doing jobs they hate? Because they're too lazy or too scared—"

"Or like to eat," Karin interrupted, giggling.

"Or aren't innovative enough," Meg continued, frowning at her, "to arrange to earn their living doing what they like to do."

Karin gave her a skeptical look. "And you're suggesting what?"

"That you quit your job and arrange to conduct art tours for profit. You know there's a need. Mrs. Trotter is quite upset that I'm going to be away a good deal and won't be able to do them for the gallery anymore. But you've helped me. You could do it. And start some daily sight-seeing tours for conferences or conventions that come into town. Now, listen . . ."

She had made it sound so simple. Uncle Bob was retiring from his job as a civilian employee at a local air force base, and he and Aunt Meg planned to use his modest pension doing what *they* liked to do—travel. It would be wonderful, they'd insisted, if Karin were to move back home, rent free, so she could be there to house-sit whenever they took off. That way, she'd have no living expenses while she was building up her business.

They had made it so easy. Meg had given Karin her lists of art devotees and had even helped her arrange the first few tours. Uncle Bob had lent her two thousand dollars for brochures and mailings. And then Mr. Turner, who lived next door, had offered the use of his bus and—

Karin sat up. Mr. Turner! She hadn't told him about his bus yet. It was too late now, and in the morning he'd be off to the high school where he taught music.

Oh, well, she would rather talk to him after she'd gone to the repair shop. Somehow or other, she had to manage something. She didn't want to give up a business she loved.

The past four months had been delightful. Lumbering through the colorful California hills, stopping now and again to allow her passengers to view the scenery and do some sketching. Even sketching a bit herself. Such freedom. And such a privilege to attend the art exhibits in places like San Francisco. She liked arranging the tours, she liked dealing with people, and she was beginning to gain regular customers. It would be dreadful to return to a dull typing job after this.

Well, she wouldn't go back. She wasn't lazy and she wasn't scared and she would be innovative. She'd think of something. She just wasn't quite sure what.

THE NEXT MORNING Karin dressed very carefully in a navy linen suit and smart navy pumps for her trip to the repair shop—and maybe the bank. She wanted to look professional and very successful. She had compiled a list of the tours she'd conducted during the past four months, as well as a list of tentative upcoming tours and projected profits. She was gathering up some of her brochures when the doorbell rang. Maybe it was Mrs. Turner

coming over for a cup of coffee. If so, Karin would just
have to break the bad news to her.

It was an express messenger who handed Karin a long
envelope. As the door closed behind him, she stared at
her name and address, neatly printed on the front. No
return address. When she tore open the envelope and
unfolded the enclosed page, a small slip of paper fell to
the floor. She picked it up.

She stared incredulously at a check made out to Karin
Palmer in the amount of three thousand, three hundred
forty-five dollars and eighty-five cents. The exact amount
she'd calculated sitting at the bar yesterday going over
and over it.

But who on earth . . . ? She glanced at the signature, a
heavy masculine scrawl. Blake Connors.

CHAPTER TWO

UTTERLY BEWILDERED, Karin looked again at the figures on the check. Amazing! This was enough, with what she had in the bank, to cover everything.

But... Her face creased in a frown. How did this—she glanced again at the signature—Connors person know exactly what she needed?

Because she had told him! He must be the man who'd said he was rich. The man with the sexy smile. She had thought he was joking and even joined in; that was the only time she'd said the figure aloud! And that was practically *all* she'd said. They'd hardly exchanged three sentences. But why would he send a check? And how did he know who she was or where to send it or... or anything?

Of course. Jake. The bus driver. He'd sat with that man at the bar while she'd assembled her people. He must have told him who she was and all about the breakdown. The man had obviously remembered the amount she blurted out and...here it was. For a moment she felt giddy with relief and gratitude. This solved her problem. There would be no need to—

Karin Palmer! Are you crazy? Nobody passes out that much money to a perfect stranger, at least not without some reason. A loan! Maybe that was it. She'd heard of these companies who sent a check—and a high interest contract for you to sign. She dug out the business card.

"Blake Connors," it read. "President. New Ventures, Inc." She tapped the card against her lip. This was probably a loan company and he'd already seen that she ran a legitimate business and was in a temporary bind. Or maybe this was a bogus check, a kind of advertisement saying she could get a loan from his company.

Desperately hoping for some logical explanation, she hurriedly unfolded the letter. In the excitement of seeing the check, it had at first escaped her notice. Hotel stationery, with Harrah's letterhead crossed out. One line, handwritten in the same decisive scrawl. "If you have further needs, I'm available. B. Connors."

Karin read the line twice and looked back at the check.

This was no loan! This was an insult. He had met a girl in a bar who had named her price, and he'd sent it by express! Her face burned with humiliation and anger. But she felt as furious with herself as with him. Spouting off about what she needed! *And when you saw that check you were eager to grab it!* Pretending it could be a straightforward business transaction. As if any businessman in his right mind would send that much money to a stranger he'd met in a bar!

Well, I'm not taking it! I don't know what you have in mind, Mr. Rich Man Connors, but I'm not for sale. So keep your money!

She started to tear the check in two, then stopped. He might get the impression that she'd cashed or at least kept it. She'd send it back, so he could have no misconceptions.

She thrust everything into her purse, planning to mail the check as soon as she'd resolved the bus problem. The anger was still there, but it was almost smothered by a keen wave of disappointment. She had seen such warmth in his smile, and something in his face had struck her as

genuine, honest. And in that moment before she'd left
the casino, a deeper emotion had tugged at her, and she
had thought . . . had wished . . . But she would not voice,
even to herself, what she had wished. She got into her car
and drove to Sacramento.

"IT'S AN OLD BUS, you know," the man at the repair shop
told her. "Been out of production for fifteen years. I'll
have to send away for an engine—if I can even locate one.
If not, we can try rebuilding it, but that's a last resort.
Probably take six to eight weeks to get the job done—less
if we're lucky."

She didn't ask about a payment plan. In fact, she felt
a little relieved. In six weeks' time she might earn the
money. Two more tours scheduled for this month and
five for next month. Of course, she'd have to lease a bus.
And that would cost five hundred dollars a trip—two
hundred more than she usually cleared!

She would be *losing* money!

She sat in her car and leaned on the steering wheel,
feeling a little numb. She couldn't raise her prices, not
after advertising and booking at her current rates. But...
She straightened abruptly. Commercial buses had a capacity for forty-six. If she could fill the bus, or even get
forty people, she could gross at least eight hundred dollars a trip!

Quickly she fumbled in her purse for the receipt Jake
had given her yesterday. Charter Lines, Inc., and an address. She put the car in gear and started for that location, her spirits lifting. Once she'd arranged for a bus,
she'd go down every tour list she had and do a masterful
job of telephone soliciting.

The man at Charter Lines shook his head. "I'm sorry."

She stared at him, uncomprehending. "I have references and I'll pay in advance if you wish." Thank goodness for that small balance in the account.

Money, he assured her, was not the problem. The fact was they had no buses available for lease on such short notice.

"Buses for commercial use," he explained, "are leased several months in advance."

"But the officer from the highway patrol got one for me immediately yesterday," she said.

"We always keep one available for emergencies," he said, "and the highway patrol takes precedence."

He seemed to sense her distress. He phoned two other companies for her, but to no avail. "Sorry," he said, again, spreading his hands. "With the casinos so close by, it's hard to keep up with the demand."

Karin thanked him and went back to her car, trying to ignore the sick feeling in the pit of her stomach. For a long time she drove slowly and aimlessly around. She couldn't operate without a bus. And whether she operated or not, she certainly had to return Mr. Turner's bus in good repair.

For the first time, she felt really scared. She might have to go back to her old job and pay for the engine out of her salary.

No! No, she couldn't do that.

All right. She'd have to cancel this month's tours. But she could reschedule once she was able to arrange transportation. She'd go home and do some telephoning, she decided—and then gave a start as she remembered the envelope that had come by express that morning, with a big check from a man named Blake Connors.

She didn't stop to figure out why her frustration should be leveled at him. Even if she dared accept the check, which she certainly had no intention of doing, it wouldn't mean a thing! And suddenly she wanted to tell him so.

There are some things money can't do, Mr. Connors! It can't find an outdated engine. It can't lease an unavailable bus. And it can't buy me!

She'd like to see his face when she gave him back his check—with a cool polite "No, thank you," just as if she had all her affairs under control!

Well, why not? She could drive over right now and return it.

It took her about twenty minutes to get to the address shown on the business card. Thirty-five hundred Forest Avenue was on the outskirts of Sacramento, and it wasn't, as she had expected, just an office. It was a whole building, a tall impressive one. She drove into the rather full parking lot and left her car in one of the unreserved slots. It was obviously a bustling place with a steady stream of people coming and going.

Connors's office was on the first floor. She felt a sense of quiet luxury when she passed through the open double doors and entered a spacious well-appointed reception room. Thick carpet, elegant furnishings in rich tones of beige and brown, lush potted plants. Everything in excellent taste.

The young man at the desk smiled at her. "May I help you?"

"I'd like to see Mr. Connors."

"Do you have an appointment?"

"No," she said. "But I..."

The young man hesitated. "Er, I'm not sure Mr. Connors is available. You'd better speak to his administrative assistant, Ms. Wentworth. Your name?" She handed him one of her cards and he whispered into the phone on his desk. Then he smiled again. "Just have a seat. She'll see you in a moment."

She started to tell him to never mind, but he'd already turned to speak to a woman in a pair of clean white coveralls with blue lettering on the back: "Dolly's Desserts." Karin shrugged and sank onto a plush sofa. Since she'd come this far, she might as well wait.

Dolly's Desserts sat beside her. She was a little plump, but pleasingly so, with a round brown face and curly black hair. She gave Karin a friendly smile, but before either of them could speak, the young man at the desk said, "Ms. Palmer, you may go in now."

Ms. Wentworth's office was not as large as the reception area but every bit as elegant. The young woman seated behind the desk might have been a model for the cover of *The Successful Female Executive*. She looked self-assured, competent and...stunningly attractive. Oval face, small well-formed mouth, delicate nose and dark luminous eyes. All this perfection was framed by a stylish crop of silky black hair cut so precisely that each strand fell smoothly into place. Karin felt an urge to go somewhere and brush her own unruly bronze curls. A soft beige jacket was draped carelessly over the back of Ms. Wentworth's chair, and her striped silk blouse with the mock turtleneck collar and large cuffs looked so crisp and fresh that Karin could literally feel her own suit wilting.

"Good morning." A slender well-manicured hand waved Karin toward a chair. "How may I help you, Ms....?"

"Palmer. Karin Palmer." Karin sat, a little irritated with herself. It wasn't like her to feel intimidated.

"Ah, yes." Ms. Wentworth looked down at a pad, obviously the information whispered through the intercom. "K. Palmer Tours."

Karin nodded. "I'd like to see Mr. Connors."

"I'm sorry. He's unavailable." Ms. Wentworth flashed a tight professional smile. "Perhaps it would be best if you saw Mr. Peterson. All new clients apply through him."

"But I'm not a new client. That is, I'm not applying for anything."

"Oh?"

"I wanted to see Mr. Connors about a . . ." Karin hesitated. She wasn't going to tell this woman about the check. "A personal matter."

"Personal?" The brows drew together. Did Karin imagine it or was there immediate hostility in those dark eyes?

"Well, not exactly."

"Oh. I see. Or rather, I don't see." Ms. Wentworth's tone implied pity for someone too stupid to know whether or not a matter was personal. Karin felt a flash of rage that focused on Blake Connors. How dared he push her into such a situation!

She stood up. "It doesn't matter. I'll just..." Mail the darn check, she finished to herself.

"Perhaps I could help," Ms. Wentworth offered. "If you'd like to leave a message." Just then a door, presumably to a connecting office, opened, and Blake Connors came out.

"Vickie, I'd like you to take care of this," he said as he walked toward her desk. Then he stopped, catching sight of Karin. "Ms. Palmer! How nice of you to come by."

"I was hoping I could see you for a minute," Karin said.

"Of course. Why don't you join me for lunch?"

"Oh, that's not necessary. What I have to say will only take a minute."

"Then you can say it over lunch." His tone was as decisive as the scrawl on his check. "Let me get my jacket."

"But you said we'd see Pete at lunch. To talk about the expansion problem with that dress exchange," protested Ms. Wentworth as he disappeared into his office.

"That's right. Forgot." He reappeared, thrusting his arms into the jacket of his lightweight summer suit, his tanned face strikingly handsome against the wheat-colored fabric. "Well, you two thrash it out. And tell Pete I'll see him at the club tonight." Apparently dismissing the matter, he turned a smiling face to Karin.

She tried to hold on to her anger. This wasn't going according to plan. But despite her better judgment, some instinct told her this man could be trusted. Anyway, she couldn't refuse the invitation. Not with Ms. Officious sitting there with egg on her face! Unavailable, was he?

"Thank you so much for your help," Karin said, giving the woman behind the desk a bright smile. She couldn't thumb her nose, but this was almost as good, Karin thought, as she walked out with Blake Connors.

IN THE PARKING SLOT nearest the building entrance, the one specially reserved for him, Blake Connors held open the door of his sleek low-slung Maserati and waited.

Karin didn't move. In fact, he thought, she looked somewhat wary. But why? When they left his office her manner had been quite complacent, even a little smug. But now...

"I thought perhaps we could walk," she said.

"Walk?"

"Someplace nearby," she suggested, gesturing vaguely toward the hamburger stand down the street. "It's so pleasant outside."

"Exactly. It would be a pleasant drive to River's End." Did she expect them to squeeze in at one of those crowded, ramshackle tables? "It's only a short way down the river road."

"Oh, no, I'd rather not," she said so quickly that he immediately caught on. Even though she glanced pointedly at her watch and explained that she was short of time, he knew that she was really saying—"I'm not an easy pickup and it doesn't take a ride down the river road to return your money."

Confirming his suspicions, Karin started to reach into her purse. "Lunch really isn't necessary. I just wanted to—"

He slammed the car door shut and took her arm. "All right. There's a coffee shop a couple of blocks from here." Before she could protest, he ushered her across the street and down the block, making polite conversation as they pushed their way through the lunch crowds. He wasn't about to let her get away. Not after the trouble he'd taken to see her again.

She had intrigued him from that first moment he'd seen her at Harrah's. He had sat there watching her try to politely ignore that jerk who'd been so persistent when she was plainly trying to thrash out some problem. He had almost laughed out loud when she finally squelched the man with a clever quip. He couldn't help joining in, and she had turned around, ready to squelch him, too. But then she'd laughed, and he'd been fascinated by the transformation. Fascinated by those deep dimples and the way her eyes had crinkled at the corners—hazel eyes that sparkled with golden glints.

He had wanted to stay beside her, to talk. But then her driver had come in, and she had jumped down and was gone. A neat little figure in that lavender jumpsuit, moving purposefully through the casino to round up her people. He liked the way she'd dealt with those ladies. It was more than professional. She had a caring way about her, as if their comfort was her only concern. She'd somehow masked her own worry and managed to transmit a feeling of tranquility, as well as festivity.

When she'd left the casino, he'd experienced a strange sense of loss. He had to see her again, and he knew the check would do it, though he'd been half-afraid she would simply mail it back to him.

Well, she hadn't, so he was in luck. Still, he thought, as they entered the noisy restaurant with its smell of coffee and frying onions, this wasn't the ideal spot to start something. He felt the need for a new diversion, and he sensed that Karin Palmer would be a delightful one. The women who flitted in and out of Blake Connors's busy life were exactly that—diversions. Since Fran. The thought of Fran, even after all these years, disturbed him, and he almost bumped into a man who was leaving. There had been no one special in his life since Fran, and he meant to keep it that way. Automatically he placed a hand on Karin's arm, pulling her toward him to shield her from the departing diners. A silky curl brushed his chin and he caught a whiff of fresh delicate fragrance before it was overpowered by the restaurant odors.

Just as *she* could be overpowered by the tough world of business. Especially *her* business. Tour runs to the casinos were a dime a dozen. She could easily go broke. He'd seen it happen many times. And that afternoon at Harrah's, she'd looked so fragile and vulnerable that he had felt an instinctive urge to protect her. Now he noticed that her brow was again furrowed in thought. Probably still worrying about her broken-down bus. Perhaps his check would solve the problem and she had decided to accept it.

But…no. As soon as they had threaded their way past the noisy crowded tables and were seated in a booth, she pulled the check from her purse. "Mr. Connors, I came to return this to you."

When he didn't touch it, she laid it on the table in front of him. "I can't imagine why you sent it."

"I thought you needed it. You said so."

She stiffened. "Mr. Connors, many people need things, which on impulse they might mention to a perfect stranger. That doesn't mean they're asking that stranger to supply them!"

"But that happens to be my business."

"Oh?" Her eyes rounded in astonishment, then suddenly danced with mischief. "Who are you? Santa Claus?"

He grinned, shaking his head. "Hardly."

"Then you must be the millionaire!"

"The what?"

"You know. The millionaire in that old TV series from the fifties. The guy who miraculously comes to the aid of a needy stranger. I heard about it from my uncle Bob."

"Oh." His parents had banned television and he'd never even heard of that series. But he understood the concept and he liked the teasing light in her eyes, the same delightful transformation in her face he'd seen yesterday at Harrah's.

"But you've shortchanged me." She grinned, tapping a finger on the check. "You see, the surprised and worthy recipient is supposed to get a full million."

"I see." His mouth twisted into a smile, but his reply was interrupted by the buxom waitress who came to take their order. When this was done, he turned to Karin. "A million is not out of the question. If you need—"

"I don't need a million dollars! I don't need anything!" she said emphatically.

"Don't be too hasty. You'd be surprised what we can do for you. New Ventures is the best incubator firm in the area."

He saw the defiance in her face give way to genuine puzzlement. "Incubator? As in eggs and chickens?"

"Sort of." He chuckled. "Only what we hatch are businesses."

She frowned. "I don't understand."

"To put it very simply, we nurture new firms through the early stages of development when they're most vulnerable, providing office space or services, access to capital, management advice—things like that."

"I see." She didn't try to veil the sarcasm in her voice. "And you pass out all these goodies willy-nilly to anyone who asks? Or even someone who doesn't ask?"

He tried to keep a sober face. "Oh, no. We're quite selective. Our clients are carefully screened and their needs precisely assessed before we take them on."

"Carefully screened," she mused. "I see what you mean. After an exchange of two sentences at a bar, you determined that I was a potentially sound client."

He lifted an eyebrow. "You were precise about the capital you needed—down to the penny."

She laughed at that and he was glad to see the tension lessen and the dimples reappear. "I'd been wrestling with those figures for most of the day," she said, "so the sum was pretty clear in my mind."

"And now you find you don't need the money, after all?"

"Yes. That is, no. I don't need it." He noticed a little tightening of her lips, which he interpreted as, *Not your problem but mine.*

"And you have no need of our expert management advice?"

Her eyes crinkled and the irrepressible dimples peeped out again. "I'm a little skeptical about that."

"Oh?"

"Expertise from someone who'd send a four-figure unsecured check to a perfect stranger?"

He gave a shout of laughter. "I assure you, Ms. Palmer, that much of my not inconsiderable success may be attributed to my keen perception and remarkable ability to read character. One glance at those big honest eyes of yours convinced me I was taking no risk."

"Ha! What you saw was desperation, and that's no character reference." She rolled her eyes. "Really, to send such a sum to a person you know nothing about..."

"Well, let's see." He folded his hands on the table and smiled at her. "Your name is Karin Palmer. You are twenty-four years old and you reside at forty-four Market Street in Carmichael with a Mr. and Mrs. Bob Palmer. On January tenth of this year, you registered your own business, K. Palmer Tours. During the two years prior to this, you shared an apartment with a Joyce Carruthers on H Street in Sacramento while you were employed at the Department of Water Resources. Your credit references, while almost nil, contain no negative information."

She shot him an incredulous look. Then her lip curled. "You forgot the lemonade stand I had when I was seven."

"Oh, no. That's what convinced me to send you the money," he said, laughing.

"Oh, stop it!" Her face reflected as much horror as amazement. "Do you know what you are? You're a sneak!"

He said nothing, but grinned while he waited for the waitress to set their cups of coffee before them. Then, as the waitress departed and a sudden uproar from the next booth subsided, he said quite amiably, "My dear Ms. Palmer, you can't have it both ways. In one breath you accuse me of carelessness in business dealings, and in another you label me a sneak for checking references."

"Oh, don't look at me like that. You know what I meant. Anyway, none of that means anything. I could easily have cashed that check this morning and skipped town."

"Instead, you show up at my office, check in hand." He raised his cup. "I rest my case."

"Oh, yes. Your case. But what about mine? What was I to think when—" She broke off as the waitress brought their food.

Here goes, he thought, hiding a smile and bracing himself for the how-dare-you lecture.

But she busied herself with her hamburger, adding catsup and cutting it into quarters, her eyes downcast, lips compressed. Then, as if shrugging off a disquieting mood, she began to eat with dainty relish and speak with polite formality. "This is delicious. Thank you for lunch, Mr. Connors."

"Blake. Can't we dispense with formalities, Karin?"

"Yes, of course." She smiled at him. "Thank you, Blake."

"That's better. Now, I think you were saying something about my case versus yours?"

"No, I... It doesn't matter." She fiddled with a French fry, not looking at him.

"I think it does. Did you believe I had some ulterior motive?"

She looked up, her face rather flushed. "Oh, no, of course not. I only—"

"If so, you were right."

CHAPTER THREE

AN ALARM BUZZED in her brain and she gave him a sharp glance.

His eyes held hers, absorbing her in a warm intimacy so compelling, it frightened her. She tried to think of something flippant to say, something that would lighten the moment. She swallowed and stared down at her plate.

"This is a good hamburger." That was flippant? And hadn't she said that already?

"Don't change the subject. I did have an ulterior motive. I want to know you, Karin Palmer."

She glanced at him sharply. "You seem to have me pretty well documented."

"Documents only skim the surface. I want to know more."

"I'm an open book," she quipped, steeling herself against the quiver of excitement aroused by the implication in his husky voice. "What you see is what there is."

"No deep dark secrets? No heart-throbbing desires?"

"Save one. My heart throbs for a bus." She tried to giggle, but a sob caught in her throat as she was jolted back to reality. What was she going to do?

"So you haven't solved that problem?"

"Not yet." Again she met his eyes. Again she had the sensation of being drawn in.

"Repair delays?"

She nodded.

"So, lease a bus. Sometimes that's better. It elimi-
nates—"

"Delays there, too."

"Perhaps New Ventures can be of service to you."

"No, I'll manage." She didn't want to talk about it,
didn't want to be exposed as a failure.

"Now, wait. Don't be so quick to turn us down. Starting a business is tough. You don't have to do it alone.
That's what business incubators are all about."

"I've never heard of a business incubator before."

"It's a fairly new concept, though we've been around
for several years now."

"We? You mean there are other companies like
yours?"

"Are we talking quantity or quality?"

"Okay. So you're tops," she said, smiling. "But you
haven't answered my question."

He chewed a piece of his—obviously tough—steak,
then swallowed. "Well, if you're in the market for a
business incubator—"

"I'm not in the market. Just curious. There are other
companies?"

"Many. And we're a fast-growing breed." He took a
sip of coffee, then leaned forward to explain. "Eighty to
ninety percent of all new small firms will fold during the
first four years of their existence. The business incubator provides a network of support that greatly increases
their chances of survival."

"But what do *you* get out of it? I mean..." She
glanced at the check still on the table. It had come gratis,
apparently no strings attached. "A welfare program for
free enterprise? That doesn't make sense!"

He chuckled as he again tackled his steak. "Oh, we all
have our motives and agendas. Many business incuba-

tors are nonprofit. Municipal governments seeking to create new jobs and increase their tax base, for instance. Universities promoting innovations they've developed, and so on.''

"And you?"

"Oh, I'm strictly an entrepreneur, in it for the profit, just like my clients. My take may be from rentals, percentage of profits or shares in the tenant company."

"Oh." She thought of his bustling office building. "You seem to have been quite successful."

"I've had 121 tenants in my eight years of operation, and only three have folded."

"You must be very good at what you do."

"I am." He grinned with unabashed confidence. "And I like it. I get a big kick out of just pointing someone in the right direction and watching him—or her—take off."

Karin listened, completely captivated by the way his mischievous blue eyes darkened with intensity as he talked about his clients. It was as if ensuring the success of each venture was a personal challenge to him. And she found it interesting to hear how he tailored his services to meet the various needs. But it was the man himself who fascinated her. So much zeal and such command of each situation. And he really cared, she thought, as he described one man who'd lost his job at a nursery because he'd hurt his back and could no longer lift the heavy plants.

"He had started a seed company in his home but wasn't making enough to pay the rent when he joined us," he said. His face lighted with boyish enthusiasm as he told how they had converted it into a mail-order firm.

"He now grosses over a million a year," he finished.

Karin, in the midst of a swallow, almost choked on her coffee. "A million! Just selling seeds?" She put down her cup. "I had thought..." She faltered. "Somehow I got the impression that you only dealt with small businesses."

"The whole idea is to grow," he said seriously. "Anyway, 'new' doesn't always mean 'small.' Some firms have to start big."

"Oh?"

"Like this woman who came to us. She'd invented a new device for drilling oil. We had to find investors, develop a worldwide market. She now has three plants."

Three plants! Worldwide market! "I thought you were joking. But you really are rich!" Darn! Why did she always blurt out exactly what she was thinking?

"I'm getting there." He sounded brusque, almost defensive. Why? What had caused that sudden tightening of his mouth, that withdrawal? The change was so abrupt it startled her. And made her curious. Suddenly it was she who wanted to know more about Blake Connors. What secret longings or deep fears rippled beneath that strong confident surface?

"Tell me about you—I mean," she amended, wanting to bite her tongue, "this business." That sounded better. "How did you get into it?"

"I drifted into it," he said. But he knew that wasn't quite the truth. He had made the move deliberately. Ed Matthews might have supplied the key, but Blake had recognized the opportunity—a move toward the goal he had set for himself on the night Fran had told him she was going to marry Ricky Dunlap, the heir to the Dunlap tobacco fortune.

"Well, now, that is a switch! Let's be clear about this." Karin was pointing her finger in the kind of kidding gesture Fran had often used to tease him out of a foul mood. Damn! He hadn't seen Fran since that night more than ten years ago. So why was he thinking of her now? The woman across from him didn't even look like Fran. She had such an open wholesome face, wide eyes. Fran's beauty was of the pale ethereal kind, with her slanting exotic eyes and long silver-blond hair. And Fran didn't have dimples. He watched the dimples dance in Karin's cheeks and tried to concentrate on what she was saying. "You drifted into a business specifically designed to prevent aimless drifting by shaky entrepreneurs?"

"Guilty, Your Honor!" He tried to laugh, tried to recapture his earlier mood. "I'd been out of school for about three years and had this nine-to-five job with a consulting firm in Philadelphia when a friend, Ed Matthews, approached me for a loan. He was operating a beauty-supply business out of the trunk of his car and had run into debt. I paid it off."

Karin's eyes shone. "I knew it. It's just in your nature to help people."

Now Blake did feel guilty. "Wasn't much of a debt," he said. "Didn't even come to a thousand. And I wasn't being entirely altruistic." He shrugged. "I knew that if I was going to get my money back, Ed had to do better than he was. So I gambled and went in a little deeper. Took out a second mortgage on my condo and bought an old warehouse. Remodeled it a bit, gave Ed storage space and some management advice that started him off in a new direction. All for a percentage of his profits, which I'm happy to say increased steadily."

"So New Ventures was launched."

"Yup. Other businesses approached me for space, and I was off!" Off to the kind of success he'd planned ever since Fran had leaned back against a booth like this one, tucked a lock of her silver-blond hair behind one ear and said, "I want more than this"—"this" being the hamburger joint with its house wine and greasy smells, the kind of place that had been a haven for them during their intimate college years. He had loved Fran. She had been like a breath of fresh air after the stuffy academic atmosphere of the flat he shared with his parents, both professors at Columbia. A wave of nostalgia swept through him as he remembered… The confidences shared as they munched French fries and onion rings, the sweet scent of her skin as they necked in the park or progressed to more intense lovemaking when he got his own apartment. He had thought it was forever—until that night. The night "forever" ended. The night he decided he might never fall in love again, but if he did, he would have more to offer than "this."

"Well, this is certainly different."

He stared at her.

"I mean your New Ventures. You've helped a lot of people succeed."

"Oh. Yes. That's the name of the game." Blake stirred uneasily. But it was true. He helped others, as well as himself.

"You're a very special person, Mr. Connors."

You'll always be special to me, Fran had said. Suddenly he wanted to get out of this hamburger joint and away from this woman who didn't look like Fran but reminded him of her.

"All finished?" he asked as he glanced at his watch. When she nodded, he said he had an appointment and picked up the bill. As he hurried toward the cashier Karin pulled at his sleeve.

"You forgot this," she said, thrusting the check he had sent her into his hand. He put it into his inside coat pocket without a word.

WHEN THEY RETURNED to the parking lot, Karin again thanked Connors for lunch and then started toward her car.

"Just a minute," he said.

"Yes?" She turned, surprised. He had hardly uttered a word during the walk back. Now it was as if he was deliberately trying to shake off a bad mood.

"This tour business of yours," he said rather hesitantly. "You were doing pretty well? Before the breakdown, I mean."

She nodded. "Very well." Then, as she saw his eyebrow quirk skeptically, "That surprises you?"

"Yes. I'd thought...well, with so many gambling tours, some of them subsidized by the casinos and—"

"Oh, my tours aren't to the casinos!"

"Oh?" Now he did look surprised. "But that's where I saw you. I mean..."

"That's just a couple of runs a month." She explained about the favor to Laura Jackson. "Otherwise I do only art tours. I've been thinking about adding theater tours, possibly to San Francisco or even to the Shakespeare Festival in Oregon. But so far I've just concentrated on art. I have two tours scheduled for next week. But now..." Her voice trailed off, the enthusiasm that had captured her for a moment dimming as she remembered her transportation problem.

"Art tours?" His interest seemed to have quickened. "That's a bit more unusual." He seemed briefly lost in thought, then he smiled. "Maybe we *can* be of service to you."

Karin shook her head. "I don't think so." She couldn't start a mail-order tour business. And she certainly didn't need an international plant, she thought, hiding a smile.

"Come into the office with me, anyway. I might be able to do something about that bus."

"Do you really think so?" she asked hopefully. "The man at Charter Lines called several places."

"Well, let's give it a try," he said, and she was glad to see his blue eyes regain that mischievous and, yes, confident look. She followed him back into the building. He led her past the reception desk into his office. The door to his assistant's connecting office was open, and Ms. Wentworth immediately called out to him.

"Oh, Blake, you're back. Good. I was afraid you'd forgotten Mr. Bryan's appointment."

"No, I'm on my way. Vickie, I'd like you to do something for me." He motioned to Karin and she came to the door of Ms. Wentworth's office. "Get Tim Holiday on the phone. Tell him I want to lease one of his buses for…" He turned to Karin. "Can you give us a list of the days you'll need it?"

She nodded and took a pad from her purse to do so.

Blake explained that Tim Holiday was a member of New Ventures. "He does gambling tours exclusively and has his own fleet of buses. I'm hoping he'll lease you one, as a favor to us."

Ms. Wentworth cast Karin a sharp glance before addressing Blake. "Ms. Palmer is a new client?"

He smiled. "Not yet. But perhaps when we show her how we can make buses magically appear, she'll be persuaded." He walked briskly into his office and returned almost at once, carrying a briefcase, and held out his hand for Karin's list. "Tim should be able to help us out," he said, passing the list to Ms. Wentworth, who frowned.

"Tim runs a tight schedule and can be hard to reach," she muttered. "I don't know—"

"I'm depending on you, love," he interrupted quietly. And Karin's heart gave an unexpected lurch as she watched him bend closer and place a familiar hand on Ms. Wentworth's shoulder. "Turn on the unfailing Vickie charm."

"Oh, you!" Ms. Wentworth, obviously pleased by his touch, smiled up at him. "I'll do my best. By the way, Pete said he won't be able to meet you tonight about that expansion proposal. He can't get together with you before noon tomorrow. I can handle it, but I need to talk to you first. Say, tonight? Your place or mine?"

So, that's the way it is, Karin thought. *Your place or mine.*

"I'll be rather late." He hesitated and Karin sensed reluctance. "I doubt—"

"That doesn't matter. And we do have a few other things to talk over. Come to my apartment. I'll make spaghetti. With your favorite sauce," she added.

"Well, I'll try. But don't bother with spaghetti." He waved to Karin. "Good luck. And remember, if you have any more problems, we're available." He opened the door, then paused to look back at Ms. Wentworth. "Listen, Vickie, if the charm doesn't work, remind Tim that I spent all of yesterday with him at Tahoe and managed to get a considerable raise in his token take from the casino bosses. He owes me." He responded to her nod with another wave of his hand and was gone.

Karin knew about the tokens given to each person in any prearranged tour group of more than ten people. The free tokens for drinks, meals and gambling were an inducement to draw customers to the casinos. She wondered how much take-back the mysterious Tim's customers received. The group she took up to the casino got fifteen dollars in gambling tokens; she charged twenty, so the round trip cost each group member only five dollars. Maybe if you owned a whole fleet of buses, your customers got their whole fare back. Big deal! In ten minutes, it was all in the slot machines, and the casino bosses knew it!

Ms. Wentworth picked up her phone. She'd assumed her former air of complacence, although Karin suspected that in reality she was anything but. She was a woman rejected—well, almost rejected. There had been that moment of unmistakable intimacy. And he hadn't said definitely that he wouldn't come. But he hadn't said he would, either. Ms. Wentworth's manner, so possessive, so eager, gave Karin the impression that she was trying to hold on to something that was slipping away. And she'd been reduced to such pleading—"spaghetti...your favorite sauce"—that Karin actually felt sorry for her. She understood how it could be. One hour with Blake Connors had shown her how easily a woman could become completely absorbed in him. But to have that closeness and intimacy and then to lose it could really be painful.

Darn! What was all this to her? She didn't intend to see the man again.

Still, if he could get a bus for her... She listened to Ms. Wentworth speak on the phone. It must be that Tim person. Well, maybe she could deal with him directly, Karin thought. Then, of course, she'd send Mr. Connors a thank-you note. Or she could come in just once to—

No! She'd seen the look on Vickie's face, heard the pleading in her voice. And after only one hour with him... Yes, he was the kind of man who could get under your skin.

She definitely did not intend to see him again.

CHAPTER FOUR

IT HADN'T TURNED OUT to be such a catastrophe, after all, Karin thought three weeks later as she set the crate of pineapples down beside the kitchen counter. This was the last day of June—half the year gone, and she hadn't had to cancel a single trip! True, the use of Mr. Turner's old bus had guaranteed an almost clear profit. But although she'd had to work like hell to do it, she'd managed to make a small profit with Tim Holiday's bus, a beautiful, air-conditioned, smooth-riding vehicle. In fact, she'd even had to turn down people for today's trip to Vikingholm. Maybe she should schedule another trip later this summer. The mansion, built in the 1920s, was situated on Lake Tahoe and faced a tiny island composed almost entirely of rocks and dotted with a great variety of evergreen shrubs. On one of its rocky elevations, the original owners had built their own private teahouse, and the site was a favorite subject for artists. Karin herself had spent much of her day at Vikingholm sketching, and after reaching home, she'd spent hours reproducing her sketches in oil.

Which was why she was now busy doing four things at once—canning pineapples, monitoring phone calls and booking reservations that came in answer to her flyers about two future tours, and drafting a flyer for a proposed trip to the deYoung Museum.

The pineapples were a must. It seemed there had been a surplus of shipments from Hawaii. So explained Rosa Lewis, who had left two crates on the doorstep a couple of days ago. "Only fifty cents apiece at the market today, so I picked these up for you." It was the kind of thing Rosa and Aunt Meg did for each other. The trouble was that Meg would still be away another week and the pineapples had to be done immediately or tossed out. Karin had just set the last sterilized jar upside down on the clean white toweling stretched across the kitchen table when a soft *yip* reminded Karin that she had another chore. She was dog-sitting Smokey, the Turners' tiny poodle. She let him out through the screen door before she turned to answer the ringing phone.

"K. Palmer Tours," she said into the mouthpiece, cradling the phone between her shoulder and chin as she selected a pineapple and laid it on the cutting board. "The Talisman Art Exhibit in San Francisco? Of course." She confirmed the pickup point and departure time while she deftly sliced the top and bottom off the pineapple and divided it into quarters. "Thank you, Mrs. Gideon. I'm glad you're coming with us. I think you'll enjoy it." She hung up the phone, wiped her hand on a dishcloth and entered the reservation for two more in her notebook. Then she husked, cored and sliced the quarters into strips, which she dropped into a big bowl. Working with her hands always stimulated her mind and quickened her thoughts. So, as she continued to slice and peel, she formulated tidbits for her flyer enticing people to attend the deYoung exhibit on July fourteenth.

"...the extraordinary watercolors depicting Native American cultures as seen by the Swiss artist Karl Bodmer, who accompanied Prince Maximilian on his 1834 exploration of the Missouri River Valley..." She paused, thinking. Yes, she had to get in the history, and she should say something about Bodmer's excellent craftsmanship—"...glowing fauna and landscape. People and customs, all anthropologically correct." And how about "... portrayed with artistic insight"?

A whine interrupted her thoughts and she dabbed her fingers on the dishcloth, then opened the screen door to let Smokey back in. A bit much to put on a flyer, but it was such an exciting exhibit. And she was lucky that Mr. Holiday was letting her use one of his buses. Of course, it wasn't only Mr. Holiday but Blake Connors who'd made this possible.

Karin didn't want to think about Blake Connors. Yet, although she had neither seen nor heard from him since that lunch three weeks ago, she couldn't stop thinking about him. The deep blue of his eyes—eyes that warmed and beckoned and drew you in. The teasing but sincere smile that encouraged you to share, to confide. The authority he exuded, that sense of command, a sheer vital power that could completely overwhelm you.

She was glad he hadn't called. Glad he'd accepted her note for what it was—a simple thank-you.

BLAKE WASN'T SURE why he'd kept the note. Perhaps because, like the woman herself, it made him chuckle. "It's worth *more* than a million," she'd written. "This beautiful, wonderful, comfortable, air-conditioned, smooth-riding bus. Never mind that it's spoiling me completely. I haven't had to cancel a single tour! Thank you, thank you, thank you. Sincerely yours, Karin Palmer." No "Come by for a drink," or "How can I repay you?" Not even a "Perhaps I might join New Ventures—could we talk about it?" Certainly none of the usual comes-ons he'd grown accustomed to.

Not that it mattered. He didn't lack for female companionship. But something about Karin Palmer was, well, different. She seemed so wholesome, and he liked her open candor, her quick wit.

Still, he probably would never have stopped by her house had he not been in the vicinity and between appointments. And in a bad mood. Mrs. Martha Channing was completely in the right to file a suit against Jack Austin, the contractor New Ventures had taken on just six months before. It was a lousy remodeling job. Nothing was right—the wiring and plumbing were slipshod, the finishing work clumsy and imprecise. Blake couldn't imagine how Austin got past the city inspectors, and he hoped Mrs. Channing would break the creep.

But of course she wouldn't. This Channing job was small potatoes to Austin, who was in the big leagues now, thanks to that extremely lucrative government contract New Ventures had helped him land. Sure, they'd cut him loose now. But it wouldn't erase the fact that they'd given a slimy cheat the boost that had launched him—which was what stuck in Blake's craw.

He was just leaving Mrs. Channing's house when he touched the crumpled note in his jacket pocket. Suddenly he was possessed by an almost overpowering desire to see Karin Palmer. To watch those dimples appear and disappear. To look into clear hazel eyes, expressive and so refreshingly honest. He was very near Carmichael. If, when he came off Eastern, he turned left instead of right...

It was a white ranch-style house set on a two-acre lot. The lawn was neatly groomed, and pink geraniums spilled from the brick planter that stretched across the front of the house. He rang the doorbell, heard the chimes resound and the violent yapping of a dog. Karin opened the door, and the dog, a small furry gray ball, continued to yap and make ferociously threatening darts at Blake's loafers until curtly chastised by Karin. "Be quiet, Smokey, or I'll put you out!"

"I was in the neighborhood," Blake explained, "so I thought I'd stop by to see how the tour business is doing."

"Oh. I . . . well, how nice." She seemed surprised and a little disconcerted. She wore denim cutoffs and a sleeveless cotton pullover that was rather stained. Her face was smudged with something that looked sticky, and her hair seemed more unruly than usual. He liked it that way, with the thick silky curls tumbling about in enchanting disarray. He was watching for the dimples when a buzzer sounded somewhere in the back of the house and she turned quickly.

"Come on back. I can't stop what I'm doing," she called as she sped away, her rubber-soled sandals tapping lightly on the hardwood floor.

He followed her slim bare legs down the hall, marveling that he'd never noticed how shapely they were. Too caught up with her dimples, he decided, grinning.

It hit him all at once—the heat, the steam and the pungent sweet odor of pineapples. It emanated from the peels spilling into the garbage pail, the slices of fruit on the cutting board and in the bowl on the counter and the jars in the wire basket Karin was lifting from a large steaming kettle.

He asked the obvious. "You're canning pineapples?"

She nodded and, using oven mitts, carefully took the hot jars from the basket and set them on the towel-covered table.

"Why?" Never in his life had he seen anyone can anything. His mother had relied on frozen goods from the supermarket and salads from the deli.

"Because they'll spoil if I don't." Now, one by one, she was placing another set of pineapple-filled jars in the rack. The phone rang. "Have a seat," she said, motioning toward a chair as she grabbed the receiver. "K. Palmer Tours." And not once pausing in her task, she talked in a calm professional voice about the departure times and pickup point for some art show. Blake looked around. The kitchen in his luxury apartment was hardly touched, and he could never remember his mother's kitchen being in such disarray. Still, there was a kind of order in this disorder, with the clean white towels spread under clean upside-down fruit jars, the big garbage can carefully lined to receive the discarded husks. And there was something strangely pleasant about it all—the persistent bubbling of water in the big kettle, the pungent odor of fresh fruit, or maybe it was just the cheerful way Karin bustled from one task to another.

By the time she'd hung up the phone, she had replaced the loaded rack in the kettle and set the timer.

"Isn't this a bit archaic?" he asked, but she shushed him while she wrote something in the notebook lying open on the counter.

"What did you say?" she asked as she laid aside her pen.

"I said isn't this—" The phone shrilled again.

"K. Palmer Tours," she said into the instrument as she picked up a pineapple and began to slice and peel. This time she pushed the notebook toward him with her elbow, mouthing, "Please." Blake, who'd been too mesmerized by the whole scene to take a chair, picked up the pen and wrote what Karin confirmed to the caller. "'Mrs.

Iola Cuthbert, reservations for four. Talisman Tour. To be picked up at Crocker Art Gallery.' Thank you, Mrs. Cuthbert,'' she finished. ''And thank you, Mr. Connors.''

''This is one hell of a way to run a business,'' he said.

She dimpled. ''I know. But I have a trip tomorrow.'' She was explaining about the unexpected delivery of the pineapples and her aunt's being away when the jars she'd set on the table began to pop.

''Something wrong?'' he asked.

''No. Right. The pop of the seal is the final touch. It means they're okay,'' she said, placing each jar that popped on the other side of the table. He started to ask about this, but the phone rang again, and the routine was repeated, he writing while she talked and chopped fruit.

''You should at least use your answering machine,'' he observed.

''Oh, I do. But sometimes people don't call back, and right now I can't afford to miss any takers. Oh, would you mind letting Smokey out.'' The dog, who seemed to have accepted Blake's presence, had moved toward the screen door. Blake opened it and let him out. He observed a large pleasantly furnished patio and a spacious fenced lawn, tastefully surrounded with shrubs and flowers. Beyond that was a swimming pool of the marble-edge vintage—not like the premolded units of today. In the distance was a vegetable garden.

''Don't tell me you garden, too,'' he said.

''Only a little.'' She laughed. ''That's my uncle Bob's department.''

''Who looks after Smokey while you're away?''

''Oh, Smokey's just visiting. He belongs to the Turners next door. They're down at Mills College for the summer theater festival. Their daughter's appearing in a play tonight. I'm glad I was home today and could keep the dog.''

"Oh?" Neighbors. This was another world he knew almost nothing about. Behind the closed doors of his various apartments, there'd been little reason or opportunity to really meet any of his neighbors. Of course you came across other occupants at the swimming pool or in the exercise room. But it wasn't this warm neighborliness—a crate of pineapples on the doorstep, dog-sitting, and . . .

". . . glad to do anything for the Turners," Karin was saying. "He lets me use his bus, you know." She described how Mr. Turner had purchased the secondhand bus several years before to transport his choir. "They were giving lots of concerts then, and he got a good deal on this bus." She knew she was talking too much, but she couldn't seem to help it. Here she was trying to seem relaxed and confident, but she was positively fidgety! Darn! Why had he "dropped by" when she was in the middle of all this and looking such a mess? Well, she didn't care. She didn't want to see him, anyway, she thought defiantly. "He said the bus was just sitting idle and I could use it for free—'just gas it up and go,' he told me. I couldn't look a gift horse in the mouth."

"Maybe you should have."

"Should have what?" Now he was standing near her, making her feel even more nervous.

"Checked the mouth. Old horses sometimes have rotten teeth. An old bus might have a rotten engine." His chuckle irritated her. She viciously lopped off a pineapple top.

"That bus served me well for four months," she said, tossing the top in the garbage pail. "It's allowed me an almost clear profit."

"Clear profit, huh? Well, let's think about that." He leaned against the counter, hands in his pockets. "You have to replace an engine. What's that? Four...five thousand?"

"No. They're rebuilding the old one." They couldn't find a new one, but that was none of his business! "It's going to cost less than three thousand." Only a few cents less, but at least she'd be able to pay for it.

"And you're having to lease buses, anyway, at around five hundred a whack."

"Yes. Thanks to you, I haven't had to cancel a single tour."

"But adding the repair costs and the leasing, are you clearing enough to cover expenses?"

"Well, Mr. Turner's bus should be repaired by the end of the month," she said, not looking at Blake as she sliced and peeled. And not answering his question. She wasn't part of his darn incubator company! Of course, he'd helped her, and she appreciated it, but there was something about his tone that rankled.

"You'll revert to the old bus?"

"Of course." What did he think? Free was free. Well, maybe it was time to start paying Mr. Turner, but that still wouldn't approach what a commercial bus cost.

"What about insurance?"

"Fully covered," she answered smugly. "The choir group had this policy for years, and it was so reasonable Mr. Turner decided to keep it in case—"

"That's not commercial insurance!" Blake said sharply. He went on to explain that there was a vast difference between insurance for nonprofit groups and commercial coverage. "You're taking a big risk," he said. Commercially chartered buses had to be fully covered by insurance with premiums that were so astronomical—he named some figures—she couldn't afford it even if she could get it.

"Oh, I didn't know that," she said a little defensively. "When Mr. Turner said he was insured—" She shrugged. "I thought insurance was, well, insurance."

"That's the trouble," he said, "with being so eager to get your business started. It means you don't do it properly. You accept handouts and depend on any Tom, Dick or Harry for advice." When you're in business for yourself, he went on at some length to explain, you have to carefully examine every aspect.

The fact that he was right didn't make it any easier to accept. Tight-lipped, she quartered the pineapple. Okay, so she should have checked the insurance out herself, but—

"You're lucky," he said, "that you just had a conked-out engine, instead of a major accident with the liabilities piling up for the rest of your life."

"All right!" she screamed. "But I *didn't* have an accident, so— Oh!" she cried as the sharp knife cut into the flesh of two fingers. She winced at the sight of blood and the sting of the acidic juice, her hand flying instinctively to her mouth.

"Good Lord!" Blake moved quickly to turn on the tap and shove her hand under cold running water. The phone rang and she half turned to answer, but he held her fast.

"Let the damn thing ring," he said. "You've cut yourself pretty badly. Where're the bandages, antiseptics?"

"Bathroom." She gestured with her head toward the hall. "First door on your left."

"Don't move," he commanded as he sprinted to the bathroom.

She wrapped a paper towel around her fingers and leapt for the still-ringing phone. Too late. Darn!

"I told you not to move," he said, returning with a first-aid kit.

"And I told you I couldn't afford to miss any calls!" she snapped. It was all his fault. If he hadn't been lecturing her, if he hadn't come here while she was in the middle of all this...

"Not as bad as I thought." He dried her fingers with a clean gauze pad and sterilized the cuts with peroxide. "I'll just make a butterfly bandage—" The timer sounded. "I'll get them," he said, stopping in his task to remove the rack of jars from the kettle and place it on the counter. "You're trying to do too many things at one time," he said as he applied medication to her fingers. "The first rule of good business is to plan, prioritize and organize. You see—"

"Will you just shut up? I had things very well organized until you barged in here and...and started in on me!"

"Started in on you?" He was smiling as he neatly cut a strip of adhesive tape to form a small butterfly bandage. The smile enraged her. "I was merely giving you a few pointers. People pay good money for such advice. My clients—"

"I am *not* one of your clients."

"That's quite evident."

"And you needn't be snide!" She felt like snatching her hand away. But he was expertly applying the tiny adhesive strips to close the gashes etched by the knife.

"This should do it," he said. "Not deep enough for stitches, thank goodness."

"Thank you," she said, somewhat mollified. "I admit I haven't done everything right, but I haven't done too badly, either. If the bus hadn't broken down..." She stopped. "Look, Mr. Connors, I do appreciate your help. But it doesn't give you the right to lecture me like I'm some misguided child who doesn't know up from down!"

"Lecture you? I was merely making a few suggestions."

"Suggestions! You pounced on me with all that talk about gift horses and insurance and... Oh, never mind!" Why was she going on like this? Because he made her feel so... so muddled. And how was she going to finish canning with one hand? Her lips tightened in frustration and she tried to remember where she'd put the rubber gloves.

"There. Just keep your hand dry," he said as he sealed the last bandage. "I'm sorry I upset you. Here, let me get rid of the battle scars. You shouldn't have put your hand in your mouth." He wet a paper towel and gently wiped her face, speaking all the while in soothing tones. "I'm sorry. I didn't mean to come down so hard on you. But that's my job, you know—organizing businesses. And that day at Tahoe... I could tell you were worried about the breakdown and yet you never let it show. To your passengers, I mean. You remained calm, cheerful, professional. I was impressed." He was so close, the blue eyes smiling down at her. She thought for a moment he was going to kiss her, and she wished... "Okay, you can answer the phone now," he said.

She hadn't even heard it ring.

"K. Palmer Tours..." She tried to keep her voice steady, tried to concentrate. She heard him open the door for Smokey, saw him peel off his jacket, discard his tie and roll up his shirtsleeves, exposing strong muscular arms as bronzed as his face. Karin imagined him standing on a sailboat or wielding a tennis racket. By the time she'd booked the reservation he was washing his hands at the sink.

"You take care of the tour business," he said as he cleared the debris from the cutting board and washed it clean. "I'll take over KP."

She stared at him. "You can't! Have you ever done this before?"

"Never. But it seems simple enough." He selected a pineapple and began to chop the fruit, whacking the first pineapple into great uneven wedges. Karin watched in some anxiety as he took charge. It occurred to her that he was trying to exhibit the same command with which he took charge of the various businesses that came under his tutelage. But he was clearly out of his depth in this home-canning business. He went at it awkwardly and with a good deal of mild cursing as he bent over the hot kettle and fumbled with hot jars of fruit. Observing his almost comedic movements, Karin vacillated between fits of giggling and surges of pure terror. Certain that a jar would be dropped, its contents and bits of glass splattered over the tile counter, she would cry out, "No, wait! Not like that...Careful! Here, let me show you."

"Damn it, get away from that steam!" he would retort. "Don't let those bandages get wet. I'm handling this."

So, making an effort to hold her breath and her tongue, she helped as well as she could between phone calls and with one hand. And she enjoyed every moment, even the teasing.

"You're back in the pioneer age," he accused.

"Wrong." She tilted her head and gave him a knowing look. "This is the era of enlightenment. We who are with it take control of our bodies, our time, our lives."

"Really? Have you considered, given your time and all, that this is more costly than those well-preserved cans on the grocery shelf?"

"Too well-preserved with all their additives," she shot back.

He quirked an eyebrow. "Aha! One of those health nuts?"

"Not exactly. It's just that my aunt Meg has a thing against preservatives."

"Enlightenment era, huh?" His grin was mocking. "And I suppose your uncle Bob is one of those chauvinistic keep-the-women-in-the-kitchen types?"

"Don't be silly." *Uncle Bob keep the free-spirited Meg anywhere she didn't want to be?* Still, Karin thought as she broke off the conversation to answer the phone, for all her freewheeling ways, Meg always managed to do whatever made Bob happy and comfortable. And he did the same for her. None of that was chauvinist or feminist or anything else, and it had nothing to do with any era. It was just *caring,* she concluded, as she hung up the phone and made note of the newest reservation. It was a personal everyday expression of the love between two people.

Another thought tugged at her, and a little smile hovered on her lips. This virile masculine presence that now dominated the room had a way of caring, too, obvious in the alacrity with which he'd doctored her cuts and taken over the canning, and yes, even in the curt commands he barked at her to keep her hands dry. He made what had always been a relatively simple task cumbersome, comic—and undeniably delightful.

For Karin the whole afternoon had taken on a special glow. She seemed suddenly more aware of the beauty of the familiar sunny kitchen, rich with the steamy sweetly pungent odor of pineapple. A strange intoxicating sensation seemed to fill the atmosphere, making her feel lighthearted, a little dizzy and incredibly happy. She was sorry when it was over, the kitchen spotless, the jars of fruit cooling on the kitchen table.

"You have to take a few jars. You've earned it," she told Blake. "Though it may turn you forever against those well-preserved cans at the local supermarket."

"You must be kidding." He gave a mock grimace. "After an afternoon like this, I'm more appreciative than ever of my friendly grocer."

"Oh, you poor unenlightened man," she teased, shaking her head. She recklessly opened one of the jars that had cooled. She fished out a strip of pineapple and held it temptingly to his mouth. "Try this on your uninformed tongue and just tell me if you can buy anything, canned or frozen, that tastes this fresh or this good."

She watched him slowly nibble the pineapple, his blue eyes fixed on hers, and once again she was immediately drawn in. She felt like a part of it all—the overpowering sensual aroma and the savory sweetness of the fruit on his tongue. She was lulled into a dreamy haze so absorbing that she was hardly aware when the fruit disappeared and her fingers instinctively lingered against his mouth. The touch of his tongue against her sensitive flesh melted something deep inside her. Strange tremors swept through her entire body, and her knees felt weak. She might have fallen had she not been enveloped by one strong arm as Blake's lips were pressed hungrily to her soft palm, teasing, promising, arousing...

"You're right," he whispered as he lifted his head to capture her gaze again. "Perhaps, though, there are greater delights to be tasted. Like this—" his lips tasted her chin "—or this..." The light touch of his lips against the corner of her mouth so tantalized Karin that she gave a little moan of protest when he drew away. He immediately pulled her close, and his arms fastened around her, molding her slender body to his. Then Blake's lips took full possession of hers. A delicious languor flowed through her, and she was conscious only of the spirals of sensation and the wonderful sound of bells. Ringing... and ringing... and ringing...

"It seems they're not going to leave." His words finally seeped through as he released her. "You'd better answer."

She was still in a daze as her hand reached for the phone.

"Not the phone," he said. "It's the doorbell."

CHAPTER FIVE

KARIN RUSHED down the hall feeling like a first-class idiot. She knew the difference between the doorbell and the phone! The doorbell chimed again. What had come over her? It wasn't the first time she'd been kissed. But never before had she been so...so carried away, as if nothing mattered but the man who was holding her, kissing her. She opened the door and blinked. Richard Ables was sitting on the edge of the brick planter looking rather dejected. He brightened when he saw her.

"I'd just about given up," he said. "Thought maybe you'd forgotten our date."

Date? What date?

"No, of course I haven't forgotten. Do come in." Richard was dressed for tennis, and then she remembered. They were to play tennis at the club. A court—had she signed for one? Everything seemed to have gone out of her mind.

"I'm a bit early," he said.

"That's all right. I'm running late. Just give me a few minutes to shower and change." And for Blake Connors to leave.

"Sure. I'll just grab a soda," he said. "It's hot out." He followed her into the kitchen and stared in surprise at Connors, who'd slung his jacket over one shoulder, apparently ready to depart. And looking as cool and composed as if he'd just completed some satisfactory business deal instead of being interrupted in the middle of a passionate soul-stirring kiss. Soul-stirring? Probably just routine for him, Karin thought, and felt a deep blush heat her face.

She introduced the two men, adding, "Mr. Connors is the man I told you about, Richard, who was so helpful when I had to lease a bus." She was annoyed with herself. Connors might think she was trying to explain or excuse his presence in her kitchen.

"Yes," Richard said. "I've heard good things about your company. New Ventures, isn't it?"

Blake nodded. "Then you might put in a word and convince Karin to join us."

"Oh, Karin can be quite stubborn," Richard murmured. "I've been trying for some time to get her involved in—" he gave a suggestive grin "—well, in a more personal project."

"Oh? Then perhaps I'd best plead my own case."

Richard threw him a sharp glance, but Blake's smile was bland. Richard shrugged and moved with a proprietary air toward the refrigerator. "Would you like a soda?" He helped himself and held out a can to Blake.

Blake shook his head. "No, thanks. I should be on my way." He smiled at Karin. "It's been a most... enlightening afternoon. Thank you."

"No. Thank *you*," she replied, trying to form a smile as composed as his.

"So long." He nodded to Richard and started for the door.

"Wait," Karin called out. "You forgot your pineapple." He retrieved his gift, thanking her again, and she watched his departure with a degree of satisfaction. No way could he look unruffled when he was carrying his coat in one arm and three jars of fruit in the other!

"Enlightening afternoon?" Richard asked.

"Home canning," she said briefly, wondering why the day suddenly seemed dull. She shook off the feeling. "Be ready in a moment. Make yourself at home." As if he needed to be told, she thought, as she hurried to the shower. Richard always made himself at home, always assumed too much familiarity.

Okay, so she'd been impressed when she first met him, a year ago. Al, her old roommate's boyfriend, had brought him over to their apartment. And yes, Richard was the type of man she admired, at least in appearance. Dark hair, dark dreamy eyes. And he was fun. They'd had some good times, the four of them—Joyce and Al, Karin and Richard. Richard and Al had shared a small house, and when Joyce decided to move in with Al, Richard had suggested he move in with Karin.

"Don't want to break up a good foursome," he said.

"Don't want to form a cozy twosome," Karin had retorted.

"Aw, Karin!" he'd pleaded. "Okay, okay," he'd quickly added, "We'd keep it strictly platonic. But you have to admit it would be practical—financially, I mean. Hey, I'm not nearly as sloppy as Joyce. And I can cook."

"Then you can manage very well on your own," she'd answered sweetly. And she wouldn't be persuaded, though they all tried.

"Really, Karin, you're behind the times," Joyce had said.

Karin thought about that now as she toweled herself dry. Was she behind the times? Living with Joyce had been fun, she supposed. But it had often been noisy and crowded, too, with something always going on. To tell the truth, she'd been glad to get back to the relative quiet of her home with Meg and Bob, glad to have time to paint and do the things she liked to do, even gardening and canning.

She pulled off the rubber glove she'd used to protect her injured hand while showering. She stared at the bandages Blake Connors had so gently applied. He had called her "archaic." Well, he'd said a lot of things. She slipped into her tennis dress and jerked hard at the zipper. Things like suggesting she didn't know how to run her own business! When, as a matter of fact, she'd been doing a darn good job. Until the engine trouble, anyway. She frowned as she tied her shoelace. Okay, there were a few things she should check into—the insurance, for instance. But she didn't need any help from Mr. Smug Know-it-all Connors!

SHE NEEDED HELP, Blake mused. And plenty of it! She was running that business like a hobby to be squeezed in between household chores and games, like the one she was about to play with that guy in his snowy white tennis togs. He didn't like that guy. Too smooth.

Still, it was just as well they'd been interrupted, Blake thought as he pulled out to pass a truck. Things had been moving too fast. Before the ground rules were made clear. He had neither the time nor the inclination for exclusive personal ties or long-term commitments, and he believed in playing fair. If he was to see more of Karin Palmer... Oh, yes, the interruption had definitely been timely.

But not timely enough, he thought, glancing at his watch. Damn! He'd missed his appointment with Silverman. And he didn't even have a good excuse. "Sorry, I got involved in a little KP." He grinned, glancing at the jars on the seat beside him. What the devil was he going to do with three jars of pineapple? All he ever consumed in his condo was a cup of instant coffee, and that only if he was running too late for his usual breakfast-bar stop. He smiled, remembering the taste, luscious, spicy and sweet. And the tempting warmth of Karin's inviting lips— A car honked and he pulled over just in time. Better keep his mind on his driving.

THREE DAYS LATER Karin hugged the phone to her ear, loving the sound of his deep husky voice, denying to herself that she had been waiting, hoping for his call.

"You're a busy lady," he said. "This is my third try."

"Oh?" She tried not to sound dubious, remembering how eagerly she'd checked her answering machine. "I must have missed your message."

"Didn't leave one. I'm allergic to machines."

"That's hardly the right attitude for an expert on proper business techniques. And weren't you telling me to use mine the other day?"

"Oh, they occasionally have their uses. But our research indicates that, personal meetings aside, the most effective mode of communication is one that seems to be fast disappearing—a real person on the other end of the wire. Someone there consistently, all the time, even when you're out of town. That one factor would greatly increase your business volume."

"And greatly increase my operating costs."

"Not if you were under our roof. You really should look us over. Besides, you owe me."

"I do?"

"Sure you do. I helped you get the buses, not to mention all that canning I did for you."

"That sounds like blackmail."

"No, indeed. Just gentle persuasion. So, can you come in on Thursday around ten? I'd like to show you around myself."

Karin stared at the rosebud in the little vase she'd put on her desk. It looked out of place amid the clutter of papers and pens. As out of place as that undeniable quiver of excitement aroused by his voice. But it wasn't the "I want to show you around myself" that decided her, or so she convinced herself. A lot of the things he said made sense, and why shouldn't she look into something that might improve her business? She ignored the prickle of warning deep inside, refused to consider whether she was really thinking of her business—or of Blake Connors.

On Thursday she wore her black linen shirtwaist dress. The simple lines gave it a classic yet casual elegance that made it worth every penny of the bundle it had cost. In low-heeled black pumps and with a tiny black leather purse over her shoulder, Karin felt sleek and smart and sure of herself as she stepped out of her car and started toward Blake Connors's office. If he asked her to lunch, she thought, perhaps to that place he'd mentioned down the river road...well, this time she'd go. Just to discuss business, of course, but her breath came short and she couldn't still the little flurry of anticipation.

"Good morning, Ms. Palmer, how nice to see you again," said Vickie Wentworth. This time she was wearing a pale peach blouse of a soft material—silk?—with a loosely fitted wraparound skirt. How did she manage to look so...appropriate and yet so feminine? She made Karin feel stiff and a little dowdy in her crisp black linen.

"Mr. Connors suggested I come in today and—"

"Yes, I know. That's all been arranged. Just have a seat." Ms. Wentworth picked up her phone and spoke into it. "Ms. Palmer is here, Pete."

Pete? Karin glanced at the closed door of Blake's private office. He'd said—

"Oh, here you are. Good," said Ms. Wentworth. Karin turned hopefully. But it wasn't Blake. "Pete, this is Ms. Palmer of K. Palmer Tours," Ms. Wentworth told the man who had entered. He was slightly built, of medium height and wore thick horn-rimmed glasses. "Ms. Palmer, this is Mr. Peterson, our operations manager."

"Just call me Pete," he advised with a pleasant smile as he shook Karin's hand. "Blake's anxious to have you join us," he said, adjusting his glasses, "so I'm to put my best foot forward. Come along."

As she followed Pete, Karin didn't look back at Blake's office. But she couldn't quell the keen surge of disappointment. Was he behind those closed doors? Or had something turned up to call him away? He'd given her the impression that— No, he had actually said it. "I want to show you around myself."

"... still available. Would you be interested in one?"

"Interested? Well, er, that is..." Helplessly she looked at Mr. Peterson. What had he said? "Sorry. All this is so strange to me."

"Yes, I know," he said. "Surprising how many people are still unacquainted with the business-incubator concept. Many a young business is lost simply because this support system is unknown."

"Yes, I can imagine," Karin murmured.

"Now, as I was saying, these first two floors contain suites for our tenant companies." He gestured toward one. "Pimbrook Insurance. As you can see, it's a fairly large suite, five rooms. But there are two small spaces still available, one room each. I think one of those would serve for you."

"Oh, I wouldn't need office space at all," she said promptly. "I have a desk and small filing cabinet in my bedroom. Quite adequate for my paperwork. Uh, I haven't actually decided... I mean, I'm not sure it would be to my advantage to join you."

"I understand." Pete smiled at her. "Take a good look before you leap. Then you can decide which, if any, of our services would be of value to you."

The thought that she might have come here more to see Blake Connors than to observe the operation made her flush with guilt. If she could get that obsessed with a man after only two meetings, it was probably best to avoid any operation connected with him!

Still, she focused all her attention on Mr. Peterson as he continued the tour. And in truth, she was impressed by the central business-support offices on the third floor. These machines and services—fax, copy machines, computers, as well as bookkeeping and secretarial services—were available to all New Venture businesses, whether located on or off the premises.

"For instance," Pete explained, "we have a gardener who works from his home, but all his business calls are handled through a telephone operator here who makes his appointments and passes on his messages."

"I see," Karin said, remembering Blake's comment about "a real person on the other end of the wire."

"Could you pick and choose which services you wish?" she asked Pete.

"Certainly," he said. "And you're billed accordingly. Didn't Vickie give you a brochure listing the options open to prospective tenants?" He seemed surprised when she shook her head. "She must have forgotten. She has a packet for you. Be sure to pick it up before you go. We have all kinds of arrangements. To answer specific needs.''

As they were leaving the accounting department, they met the same woman she'd seen that first day in the front office, Dolly's Desserts still emblazoned on her crisp white coveralls. Now Karin discerned that she was in her late thirties or early forties.

''Mrs. Spencer,'' Pete greeted her. ''How are things going?''

''Couldn't be better,'' she replied in a cheerful voice.

''Good,'' said Pete. ''Then you're just the person to talk to Ms. Palmer here. We're trying to persuade her to join us.''

''Listen, it's worth it just to be able to dump these.'' The woman held up the sheaf of papers she was carrying and smiled, small even teeth gleaming white against her smooth dark skin. ''I leave the bookkeeping to the experts. I'm no good at figures.''

Pete explained that Dolly Spencer was the proprietor of a bakery located in Complex One. Perhaps, he suggested, Dolly could show Karin those facilities. ''That is,'' he added, ''if you'd like to see them.''

Karin decided she would. She had no need for more space, but she was curious. Now that she was inspecting New Ventures, she got the feeling that the operation was as caring and personal as it was mammoth. And she'd like the opportunity to discuss the incubator project with Dolly Spencer, and perhaps some of the others, to see how they felt about it. And about Blake Connors.

''I look forward to having you with us,'' Pete said as he left them. ''Don't forget to pick up your packet from Vickie.''

Karin said she wouldn't, and, thanking Pete for showing her around, went off with Dolly.

"I hope you don't mind the walk," the other woman said. "I never drive over. I need the exercise."

It was only about a two-block walk to Complex One. This building, Dolly told her, contained the businesses needing operational space, such as Carlson's Packaging and Delivery service, Dolly's Desserts and the like.

"How long have you been with New Ventures?" Karin asked.

"I joined almost seven months ago, about a year after my husband died. I was just muddling along by myself, hardly making ends meet. But now...well, sometimes I think I'm getting too big for my britches. Mr. Connors started me off in a different direction and it's been great."

This was something Karin was to hear often as she toured the facilities. "Mr. Connors says...", "Connors suggested..." or "Before we joined Connors, we never..." It seemed that each person's business had expanded or improved, and all credit was due to Blake Connors. Karin thought of the conversation when he'd taken her to lunch, his blue eyes sparkling with zeal as he talked about his clients. Each case was clearly a personal challenge to him. She admitted now how much she'd looked forward to seeing him. She swallowed, trying to stifle the persistent feeling of disappointment.

"And this is my corner," Dolly said as they entered the first of two rooms, an office area modestly furnished with a small conference table and chairs. "Just have a seat and we'll have some coffee as we talk. But I need a word with Sally—my assistant—first. And I want to check on Keith." She opened the large door to the second room. The fragrant aroma of baking streamed into the office, along with the sounds of oven doors opening and closing, the clatter of baking sheets and the whirring of a machine that kneaded dough.

"I really should be going," Karin said, glancing at her watch.

"Oh, please stay for coffee. I want you to sample a new item we're marketing, an apple tart. And you might like to talk to Jane Morris, the newest member of our complex. She's in the software business, which—as I've so recently learned—touches all of us business people. I'll be back in a moment." She disappeared into the wonderful-smelling room.

Karin took a chair and glanced idly at the loose papers lying on the table. Someone had been doodling. And rather excellent doodling, Karin thought as her artist's eye scanned various sketches of a dog.

"Who's the artist?" she asked when Dolly returned with a tray of tarts.

"Oh, that's Keith, my son. Can't sit down without a pencil in his hand. And here's Jane, just in time. I'll get the coffee. These are right out of the oven and they're delicious, if I do say so myself."

"You don't have to advertise," Jane said, laughing as she brought over mugs of coffee. "It's bad enough working next door to the tantalizing aroma of all those goodies. I've already gained four pounds."

"Oh, hush, and I *am* advertising," Dolly said. She sat next to Karin and advised her to "just have a taste." When Karin complied, Dolly went on, "Perfect to serve with morning coffee to a tour group, don't you think? Why do your own baking when you can get home-baked goods from Dolly? Now, aren't these good?"

Karin nodded and smiled her agreement. After ten minutes with Dolly she had discovered that you didn't talk, you just listened. Dolly had been one of the most effusive in her praise of Blake Connors and soon reverted to the same subject.

"My husband and I were caterers. Doing private parties and the like. But my desserts were always a hit, and Mr. Connors said, 'Why don't you specialize, Dolly? And make your specialty your selling point.' So I did just what he said and sent some samples to the various hotels. Now I'm supplying all the desserts at three big hotels in Sacramento. I'm also thinking about frozen pies and cheesecakes—you know, getting a line in with one of the grocery chains. Mr. Connors suggested that, too."

"Yes, he does have good ideas," said Jane. "Best thing I ever did was join New Ventures. And I met my fiancé here," she added, flashing the diamond on her left hand. "Jack Austin. He's a building contractor. He was doing just some small remodeling jobs, but Blake Connors taught him how to compete, and he's since landed a government contract. Not a big one, but he's bidding on another one right now, and if he gets that, he's really in. Oh, hello, Keith."

"Hi," said the tall good-looking boy who had just emerged from the kitchen.

"This is my son, Keith," Dolly said. "Keith, this is Ms. Palmer."

"How do you do?" Keith said politely, but before Karin could compliment him on his excellent drawings, he'd murmured, "Excuse me," and turned to his mother. "Mom, I'm finished. Can I go home now? I could catch the bus." There followed a brief exchange between mother and son, the son obviously disgruntled when his mother insisted, "Wait until I'm ready to go. Now, if you finish packaging that last order, we can leave a little sooner." When the boy departed, Dolly faced the other women with a sigh.

"It's hard for him," she explained. "Hanging around here all summer when he'd rather be out with his friends. But he's barely fifteen, and unless I'm home or he's got a program . . ." Her eyes were troubled as she gazed after her son.

"Jack says if he gets this next contract we'll go to Europe for our honeymoon," Jane confided, still immersed in her own concerns. "I'm already lining up another worker, and my sister says she'll help out. Best to have someone you can trust if you're going to be away, you see. Jack's partner . . ."

Karin wasn't listening. The boy had looked so sad. . . .

AT THE FRONT OFFICE Pete told Vickie Wentworth that the Palmer woman had walked down to Complex One with Dolly Spencer. "She'll be back to pick up some brochures," he added. "I thought Blake left a packet for her."

"Oh, that's right. I believe he did," Vickie said in a careless voice. "But surely he can't be thinking of taking her on. We already have Holiday's outfit. Another tour company would be competition—or at least excess baggage."

"Sometimes it ain't the baggage, but the baggager!" Pete grinned. "Anyway, Blake seems anxious to impress Ms. Palmer, so make sure you give her the info."

Vickie nodded, frowning thoughtfully as she watched Pete leave.

Five minutes later Blake Connors rushed in. "Did Karin Palmer get here?" he asked.

"Oh, yes, some time ago," said Vickie. "Pete gave her the grand tour."

"And you told her I'd be back in time for lunch?"

"Well, I meant to, but..." She spread her hands. "She seemed in such a hurry."

"Oh?" Blake was surprised at his own disappointment. He checked his watch. "I made reservations at River's End. Better call and cancel, Vickie."

"No, let's not cancel. This might be a good chance for us to talk privately. Honestly, Blake, things are so hectic around here and there are some issues we need to discuss—quietly. We got a letter from Austin's lawyer. He says we don't have just cause, that we can't dump him."

"The hell we can't!"

"Well, there are a lot of ramifications. I need to fill you in. And we'd better go where we won't be interrupted. Look, let's get out of here before another horde arrives."

Blake shrugged. He *was* hungry. Might as well eat while they sorted things out.

IT MIGHT BE A GOOD IDEA to join New Ventures, Karin mused as she walked away from the complex. She'd felt so comfortable sitting there with Dolly and Jane. And even though Dolly dealt almost exclusively with large orders for hotels and banquets, she said she'd be happy to supply Karin with small quantities of fresh-baked goodies for her tour groups. That would be a real time-saver, since Karin often made her own cookies and muffins. Yes, belonging to New Ventures would be like belonging to a big family. And they said those regular management meetings were really productive, with ideas and suggestions tossed around that maybe you'd never thought of. Running a business by yourself could be pretty lonely. Here, there was togetherness, as well as independence. She'd just stop by Blake's office and pick up those brochures. If he was there... She wouldn't ask, but if she did see him... Once again that tantalizing feeling of expectancy stirred within her.

She had rounded the corner of the building and started toward the entrance when she saw them. Two figures, a man and a woman. Karin was some distance away, but she recognized that sexy peach blouse with the wraparound skirt. Vickie was walking very close to Blake and he was looking down at her intently. Karin stood quite still, watching them get into his car and drive away, their heads close together. Like lovers...

CHAPTER SIX

BLAKE CAREFULLY maneuvered the Maserati between the rows of parked cars, masking his irritation when Vickie leaned closer to place a hand on his leg. He liked Vickie. Moreover, he appreciated her business acumen and realized she'd been invaluable in the development and smooth operation of New Ventures. But when it became apparent that Vickie desired more than a business relationship, Blake had tactfully tried to withdraw. He'd curtailed those private planning sessions held over lunch or dinner, and always made sure that Pete was along. So how, he thought with exasperation, had he allowed himself to be roped into this little tête-à-tête? If only Karin had waited. He'd cut out before the Chamber of Commerce meeting was over and ... He chuckled. Was he actually blaming Karin for not being here to protect him from his own assistant?

"It's not funny. This is serious business," said Vickie.

He shot her a quick glance, trying to figure out exactly what she was talking about.

"And, honestly, Blake, I think you're making a big deal out of nothing. Just because some fussy old woman filed a complaint about a two-bit job—"

"I checked," Blake said tersely. "There were flaws in Austin's contract with Channing. Fine-print flaws that had to be deliberate. I don't like dealing with a cheat."

"Oh, I agree with you. But you're going to have to deal with his lawyer. And think about this, Blake. He's put in a bid for the new City Library, and apparently he's got a good chance of winning. We've made quite an investment in his development, and I don't like to see us lose out just when we're on the verge of realizing a profit. Look, why don't you have another talk with Jack?" she said persuasively as her hand slowly caressed his knee.

"Nope. I'm through talking." He took her hand and gave it a gentle squeeze before casually placing it on the purse in her lap. "You have a good sound business sense, Vickie, and usually I trust your judgment. But this time I have to rely on my instincts. Austin's out," he said with finality.

"Well, I hope you know what you're doing." Vickie folded her arms and shrugged. "But if you ask me, I'd say you were tossing out the goose just before it lays the golden egg."

"Golden, maybe. But more than likely rotten, and it won't be hatched by me." Again he chuckled as he thought of Karin's remark. *Incubator? As in eggs and chickens?* she'd asked as those dimples danced in her cheeks. "I'm sorry you let Ms. Palmer get away," he said now. "I wanted to talk with her."

Vickie's lips tightened. "I'm not Ms. Palmer's keeper. And if she was in a hurry..." She raised her hands, palms up. "I don't understand, anyway. Surely you aren't thinking of taking on another tour business. Tim Holiday—"

"You forget. Tim's on his own now. Or he will be as soon as we arrange financing for his plane tours to Monte Carlo."

"Still, I think he'd be pretty upset at our sponsoring a competitor."

"Oh, come off it, Vickie! How could he be upset? When we took him on, he was running a bus to Reno twice a week. Now he's got a good hook-up with the casinos, and he's running about five buses a day, plus several to Las Vegas. Not to mention the Monte Carlo project. What Tim does with gambling, Karin can do with art. That's her specialty."

"Really?" Vickie grimaced. "I suppose you visualize regular tours to the Louvre in Paris and perhaps a few to Amsterdam and the like! Or are you counting on the high interest in fine arts in the Sacramento area?"

Blake didn't miss the sarcasm in her voice, and he stirred uneasily in his seat as he drove into the restaurant parking lot. Privately he'd wondered if there was enough interest to sustain a tour company dealing exclusively in art. And, damn it, piling a bunch of people into a beat-up old bus with no insurance! No business sense at all!

But she had spunk and enthusiasm and that radiant heartwarming smile...

"Well, are we going in to lunch or are we just going to sit here in the parking lot?"

Blake started guiltily and switched off the engine. "Right. Let's eat," he said rather vaguely. Art. A narrow field. If she was to make a decent profit, she'd have to find some way of supplementing—

"Well, are you coming?" Vickie's voice was sharp.

"Coming," he answered as he pocketed his keys and followed her into the restaurant.

"No, IT'S NOT LIKE a consolidation," Karin said the next morning as she sat at breakfast with her aunt and uncle. They had returned the evening before, and she was anxious to sound them out about New Ventures. "He calls it a business incubator."

"Never heard of such," said Bob, adding two spoonfuls of sugar to his coffee while Meg's attention was focused on the melon she was tasting.

"Not good," she decided. "I should have taken it back."

"But the nectarines are delicious," Karin said, selecting a slice from the variety of fruits on her plate, the usual breakfast menu ever since Meg had adopted a dietary doctrine that prescribed nothing but fruit until noon.

"So how does this incubator thing work?"

Karin explained as best she could. "As you can see," she concluded, "each company receives advice and assistance, but remains independent."

"Independence, that's the key." The lace on Meg's turquoise housecoat fluttered as she waved her hand. "Do you know they're advising that some foods be eaten independently now? Like melons or bananas—they should always be eaten alone."

"In private, you mean?" Bob asked, winking at Karin.

"Don't be silly." Meg tossed her head. "I mean, not mixed with any other food. Strange. People have been putting bananas on their cereal for ages." She frowned as if considering the idea. Then she shrugged. "Well, it's not good to just pick up any newfangled idea. One should think independently. What are you going to do, Karin?"

"Do? About bananas, you mean?"

"No, silly girl. About this company. Are you going to join?"

"No. Well, I don't actually know," Karin said hesitantly. Even now she could feel it—that dizzying jolt sweeping through her at the sight of Blake with the Wentworth woman. It wasn't jealousy, though! A warning maybe? Karin had climbed into her car and firmly turned her back on New Ventures. But then last night when he'd phoned... "I—I'm not sure if I ought to join."

"What do you know about this man Connors?" Bob asked.

"Not very much." Why did she feel she'd known him forever? "As I told you, I just met him."

"Hmm," Bob mused. "In a bar. And he's been pressuring you ever since."

"Oh, no, he hasn't been pressuring me! He helped me get a bus and—"

"And he's been out here, had you down to his place and phoned you last night."

"But he didn't say anything—about business, I mean. He just invited me to go out to dinner with him tonight."

"That was nice," said Meg. "Is he a nice man, Karin?"

"Yes, he—"

"What's he asking up-front?"

"Up-front?" Karin stared at her uncle.

"How much does it cost for you to join?"

"Oh. Nothing. As I understand it, you pay a rental fee or a certain percentage of your profits. I, uh, didn't get the details." She hadn't even bothered to pick up the brochures.

"Aha! That's the way these scams work. No details at first. With some big giveaway as the come-on. And before you know it, you're doing all the giving and they're doing the getting."

"Oh, no! Blake... Mr. Connors isn't like that." She was glad she hadn't mentioned the check. "I don't want you to think—"

"You'll probably get the big pitch tonight." Bob pushed back his chair and stood up. "But don't you sign a thing. Not until I look it over."

Living with her uncle, thought Karin, did have its drawbacks.

"Just a minute, Bob," said Meg. "Karin may be your dear brother's only daughter. But she's big enough now to make her own decisions."

"Of course. But two heads are always better than one. I'm just combining our thoughts." He leaned over to tweak his wife's nose. "As you do your peaches and pears, my pet."

"Don't be silly." Meg slapped his hand. "We're talking about two entirely different things, and you know it." She turned toward Karin, her eyes bright with interest. "This Mr. Connors, Karin. He's a young man? Handsome?"

BLAKE WAS SURPRISED that evening when the door at 44 Market Street was opened not by Karin but by a rather small man with thinning gray hair.

"You're Blake Connors?" the man asked, squinting suspiciously at him.

"Why, yes," he said. "I think Karin is expecting me."

"Of course. Come in." The man moved aside for him to enter. "I'm Bob Palmer, Karin's uncle. I'm glad you're a little early. I wanted to talk with you. Come on in."

Blake followed him into the living room, disconcerted by a feeling somewhat reminiscent of one that had plagued him years before when facing an inquisition by a teenage girl's anxious father. The big round table was cluttered, no longer with jars of fruit, but with other paraphernalia—boxes of slides, albums, piles of brochures and photographs.

"Hello," said the woman seated at the table. "Oh, my! Yes, indeed you are!"

"Er, yes, Blake Connors," he said, covering his confusion at her words and obvious scrutiny. "How do you do?"

"Fine. I'm Meg, Karin's aunt." Although her green eyes sparkled with youthful brilliance, the corners were crinkled with tiny lines that suggested years of laughter. Her hair was short and black, save for a snowy white streak at the temple, so striking he wondered if it was natural.

"Sit here, Mr. Connors." Bob pulled out a chair for him. "If you don't mind, I have a few questions that—"

"Oh, Bob, do give the man a chance to breathe. Karin will be ready in a moment. Would you like a drink, Mr. Connors?"

"Thank you." Blake sat and gestured toward her drink, which appeared to be scotch. "Whatever you're having."

"Good." Meg moved quickly toward the refrigerator in the adjoining kitchen, and Bob seated himself at the table beside Blake.

"Now, Mr. Connors," he began in a voice that was half apologetic, half confiding. "I hope you don't mind, but I'd like to have a few things made clear. Karin has been in my care since she was a child, and I guess I'm in the habit of protecting her."

"Of course." From what, for Pete's sake? After all, Karin was twenty-four years old. Did the man think he was some kind of jerk about to take advantage of her?

"Here you are," said Meg, setting a glass and napkin before him. "Brewed from rice bran and a special herb tea. So refreshing, and good for you, too."

"Thank you." Blake took a small sip and managed not to grimace.

"Now, Mr. Connors, just what do you have in mind?" Bob asked, and Blake gulped at the implication in his voice—*Declare your intentions, young man!* Rather outdated, but kind of touching, all the same.

"Have you ever been to Hawaii?" Meg asked.

Blake nodded. "Several times."

"Isn't it the most incredibly beautiful place in the whole world? All those fantastically colorful flowers— plumeria, water lilies, bougainvillea, orchids. A veritable kaleidoscope. I'm thinking of concentrating on reproducing flowers in oils if I can—"

"Later, Meg," Bob pleaded.

Meg, who had returned to her task of sorting slides on the board in front of her, paid not the slightest heed to her husband. "Come over here and look at these. Aren't they positively gorgeous?"

"Spectacular!" Blake said as he stood looking down at the bright array of blossoms illuminated on the lighted board.

"The thing is, they grow in such abundance," Meg continued. "The more you pick, the more they multiply. You can take and take and take and never diminish the supply."

"Speaking of which," Bob broke in firmly, "just how much is it going to take for Karin to get into this business and what exactly will she get out of it?"

Blake stared at him. Business. The man's skepticism concerned New Ventures. And he had thought... The joke was on him. He wanted to laugh out loud, but he managed a sober smile. "Just a minute," he said to Bob. "I have some information in the car that might interest you."

When he returned with his briefcase, Karin had at last surfaced. She wore a pale green dress, possibly silk. No frills. A simple sleeveless dress that didn't cling yet somehow managed to emphasize the slender perfection of her figure. It flared a bit at the knees, exposing tanned shapely legs.

"Hello," she said, smiling shyly.

"Hello." He caught his breath. Karin. Bronze curls, brushed smoother than he liked, pert slightly turned-up nose, wide hazel eyes. And those dimples, appearing with that radiant wholehearted smile. He felt a sensation of warmth, almost of serenity. With a shock, he suddenly realized why he'd misconstrued her uncle's questioning. Because not once during the drive out here had Blake thought of New Ventures, or the tour business, or anything except the woman he would see. And now all he wanted to do was whisk her away from her zany aunt and suspicious uncle.

"Take this chair, Karin." Bob swept aside several of Meg's folders to clear a space on the table for Blake's papers. "Mr. Connors is going to explain his proposition, and you ought to be in on it."

"I should think so, since it's her business that would be affected," Meg whispered. At least that was what Blake thought he heard before he resignedly returned to his chair and opened the briefcase.

"The business incubator is an increasingly popular economic support tool designed to foster the growth of new businesses," he began. "It increases their chances of success by eighty to ninety-five percent. Now, at New Ventures, we specifically..."

Karin sat beside Blake and marveled at the mastery with which he held her uncle spellbound. Of course these were the same traits that had so captivated her that first day—the magnetic charm, the enthusiasm, his genuine concern for the people he dealt with. And now there was more. Now there were precise details of businesses launched, businesses saved, lives turned around. Dynamic accomplishments backed by statistical data and documentation that Blake pulled from his briefcase, leaving Bob unequivocally convinced.

"Oh, yes. I see. I see," her uncle kept saying. "You should definitely go for it, Karin. Okay, you'll need what services…" He picked up a pencil ready to list her needs and potential fees. To her surprise it was Blake who demurred.

"Perhaps you should first check my credentials with the Better Business Bureau. If she wants to, Karin can come in one day this week and we'll go over everything then." Blake glanced at his watch. "We don't want to miss our reservations," he murmured.

Karin, who had been as impressed as her uncle, was still in a kind of euphoria as Blake led her out. The air was warm and heavy with the sweet scent of summer flowers, now bathed in the golden glow of the late-setting sun. She felt the strength of the hand that held hers. A hand that cleverly and unerringly guided so many to the success they craved. She looked up at his rugged features, her gaze focusing on the firm mouth that curved as if always on the edge of laughter. At the same time, though, it signaled a calm assurance that made her feel … protected, she supposed. The feeling was so new, so strange, she couldn't really put it into words yet.

"It's quite remarkable what you do at New Ventures," she said. "I know Bob was—" She broke off as Blake stopped and lowered his head to brush her lips with his, hardly touching, but with such tenderness that she was aware only of his nearness and the thudding of her heart.

"Enough of New Ventures." His voice was a husky whisper, but the promise was as definite as the prolonged chirping of the cricket that sounded far, far away. "Tonight belongs to us."

CHAPTER SEVEN

THERE WAS A GRACIOUS elegance about the Cedar Room, an elegance of candlelight, carnations and crisp linen. It was quiet, the music soft, tables spaced so that you could hardly hear the muted voices of other diners or the rattle of china and crystal.

Karin had dined there before, with Richard. She'd listened to the same tunes by the same combo, danced.

But tonight was different. She felt buoyant, keenly alive, poised on the edge of some secret bliss. Though barely conscious of what she ate or drank, she was acutely aware of every feature of the man across from her. Every nuance of expression was to be stamped forever on her memory—the questioning quirk of an eyebrow, the ironic twist of his mouth, the way his deep blue eyes could narrow with intensity or twinkle with amusement. She was also aware of the way he looked at her, and the admiration in those blue eyes both warmed her and imbued her with confidence. She felt beautiful, clever and witty, and she behaved with a provocative audacity quite uncharacteristic of her.

"Tonight belongs to us," she reminded him, a teasing note in her voice. "So let's begin with you."

"Begin?"

"Tell me all about yourself."

"Oh. Well . . . before starting New Ventures I worked as a consultant for—"

"No, no, no." She shook her head vigorously. "We've already covered the rich-man-poor-man bit. I want to know the *real* you." She leaned forward. "I don't have access to the spies or whatever agents you employ to dig into the personal affairs of a random acquaintance. So I'm left completely in the dark."

"Oh?" There was that amused quirk of an eyebrow.

"Oh!" she mocked. "Do you realize I don't know if you're married, divorced or—" she playfully wrinkled her nose "—living in sin? Or if you have any ties, legal, moral or otherwise to some charming female who might take issue with ... this kind of pleasant interlude?" She managed a suggestive wave of her hand, but her heart turned over as she thought of Vickie Wentworth and waited for his answer.

"Come to that, I'm as much in the dark as you. What about that tennis player ... what was his name?"

"Richard? Just a friend." She pointed her fork at Blake. "You're skirting the question!"

He laughed. "Okay. No ties and no commitments, legal or otherwise, and no plans for any in the near future. I have many friends, however, and I enjoy the company of women. I enjoy—what did you call it—'pleasant interludes' and—"

"Never mind. I get the picture." She pretended to make a note with the handle of her fork. "Swinging bachelor with a roving eye."

"Now wait! That's not fair. I only meant—"

"Objection sustained. Strike that remark," she said, laughing as she speared a scallop and began to enjoy her dinner. No ties. "Anyway, I only wanted to clear the record. What I really want to know is where you were born, where you went to school, what position you played in Little League—things like that." She spoke casually, hoping she didn't betray how desperately eager she was to know every detail of his life.

"Back to basics, huh?" He cut into a juicy slab of prime rib. "Okay. I was born at University Hospital in New York, lived in a flat near Columbia where both my parents taught, and I didn't play Little League."

"So what did you play?"

"My dad and I used to work out at the gym. And at prep school I was on the swim team. But mostly I had to stay glued to the books. Not that it did much good." He grinned. "I think my folks thought they'd brought the wrong kid home from the hospital."

What she drew out of him was told matter-of-factly, even with a touch of humor, and Karin had to read between the lines to fully understand. His parents were both professors at Columbia University, both Phi Beta Kappas who had seemed bent on making a whiz kid of their only son. Actually he'd been quite privileged—private schools and lots of travel. He made her laugh as he told anecdotes about the two years in Russia while his father studied the language and the year in Greece when his mother was on a fellowship. Still, she sensed that for him those early years had been more work than play. And lonely, she thought.

He seemed not to want to talk about the college years.

"That's enough about me," he said as he led her to the dance floor. "I'd rather hold you in my arms."

It was as if the sharing had drawn them closer, and she felt a new tenderness, a magic promise in the way he held her, his breath tickling her ear. As she matched her steps in perfect rhythm to his, a warm glow of joy spread through her and she didn't want the evening to end. When, long after midnight, they reached her house and he bent to touch his lips to hers, she found herself clinging to him.

"Let's go swimming," she said on impulse.

"What?" He drew back, giving her a startled look.

"The night's warm and the pool's heated—just waiting for us," she said provocatively. "You said you were on the swim team. I want to see you perform."

He laughed. "I'm not exactly dressed for the part. And though I'm not averse to skinny-dipping I think your uncle might have some objection."

"Don't be silly," Karin said, much in the manner of her aunt Meg. "We always have attire for guests."

"Okay, I'm game." He sounded eager, then hesitated. "What about your aunt and uncle?"

"Meg and Bob? Their bedroom's on the other side of the house. Even if they heard, they'd be more likely to join us than complain." She was lucky, she thought, to have landed an uncle and aunt who were always ready for fun. "Come on," she said, and took his hand.

KARIN STOOD BY THE POOL, feeling the enchantment of the night. It was so still and yet so strangely alive with the echoing song of crickets and the twinkling of stars from above. Even the full moon seemed to twinkle. Its light filtered through the trees, casting a silvery gleam on the water of the pool and clearly outlining Blake's beautifully proportioned physique. As he took a purposeful step toward her, Karin was suddenly aware of her own bikini-clad figure, and her breath caught. She sensed a warning to stifle that warm glow smoldering deep inside—quickly, before it could burst into uncontrollable flame.

"Last one in is a toad," she called, resorting to a childish game played many times around this pool. "One for the money, two for the show, three—"

"—for what I've been wanting to do all evening," he finished as his arms closed around her. "Do you know what an enticing creature you are, Karin Palmer? How hard it is to sit across from you and talk sensibly when all I want to do is this?" He slowly caressed her waist and Karin thrilled to the touch of his hand on her bare skin. "And this," he said, rumpling her curls. "I like you tousled and sticky with the sweet taste of pineapple on your lips." He tilted her chin. His eyes were illuminated in the moonlight, and she felt as if she were drowning in their depths, hypnotized by the steady gentle fingers that continued to caress her midriff. She ran a hand along his chest, then tightened both arms around his neck, drawing him closer. She heard his sigh of satisfaction as he traced kisses along her temple and nibbled at her ear, sending small currents of desire rippling through her. "So beautiful, so desirable," he murmured.

"Oh, Blake. Blake. I want…want…" Her voice trailed off as she arched her body to his.

"So do I, my sweet. So do I." His lips captured hers with such possessive demand that she trembled with need, an unfamiliar passion throbbing through her. His caressing hand tenderly brushed her stomach and she gave a little moan, consumed by a hunger so voracious, so compelling, that she wanted only to give…to love…

Love. The thought jolted her back to reality. This wasn't love. This was… In sudden panic she broke away from him.

"Karin?" She heard the puzzled confusion in his voice as he moved toward her. She stepped back, feeling exposed and vulnerable. Scared.

"I . . . I thought we came out here to swim," she managed before turning and plunging into the pool.

The water was like a slap in the face, and she choked and sputtered before she dived under, wanting to hide. Now she felt silly and incredibly naive. What must he think of her? He was accustomed to sophisticated women, like that Vickie Wentworth who—

"Last one across eats worms!" He slipped into the water and swam past her.

Happily relieved, as if exonerated from her childish behavior, she joined the race, arriving at the other edge several seconds after him.

"Unfair," she gasped. "You didn't count properly. And besides, you're taller than I am."

"Okay," he said. "I'll give you a head start. Get set . . . ready . . ." She shot out, but he caught her by the ankle. His firm grip sent a spiral of pleasure racing through her, and she felt an excited expectancy as he pulled her back. This time when he kissed her . . .

"Not *that* much of a head start," he said, instead, with a teasing scowl. "You have to wait for the count."

For an hour they cavorted in the pool, racing above and below the water. They floated on their backs and gazed at the stars. They sat on the marble edge, dangling their feet in the still-warm water, and sipped sodas from cans. Talked. And all the while Karin tried to recapture their earlier mood. If he looked at her in that certain way, made her feel confident and desirable . . . If she could only be daringly provocative, flirtatious . . . But he didn't and she couldn't. He seemed distant, somehow, and she felt shy.

"Have you always lived here?" he asked.

"Since I was ten." She told him of her parents' deaths, the kindness of Meg and Bob. Yes, she answered, she had found the government job dull. Yes, she loved art, and there was something challenging about having her own business. Yes, she did want to make a success of it.

He said he could help her do that.

But Karin wasn't thinking of art or business. She was still lost in the enchantment of the night, the whispered promises echoed by the crickets' singing, the heady erotic aroma of Meg's jasmine plants. She was thinking of the man beside her, remembering his arms about her, remembering his touch. She was waiting.

But he didn't kiss her again. Not once.

"YEP. I THINK you did the right thing, getting into that incubator business," Bob said three weeks later as he set a small cooler on the kitchen table and prepared to pack the lunch he and Meg would take with them on a motor trip down the coast. He began to line the cooler with ice and grinned at Karin, gesturing toward the phone. "Now that your calls have been switched down there, at least we don't hear the damn thing ringing every few minutes."

Karin dimpled. "And Ruth, the telephone operator at New Ventures, is so good at her job. Usually she has every space on the bus booked—even though I have to share her with four other businesses!" Karin had been a little wary at first, afraid of losing control of her own business. But being a part of New Ventures had actually made things easier.

She set a container of deviled eggs beside a stack of sandwiches and shook her head. "Are you sure you have enough? You'll be on the road all of four hours," she teased.

"With Meg stopping at every vista point? Six hours at least. And I have to do something while she sketches— like eat."

"Karin, do you mind if I take these?" Meg came in holding two bottles of champagne. "We can open them tonight when we meet Dave and Joan at the beach house."

"Take all you want. I won't be needing them."

"But I thought you served it on the trips back to town."

"Not anymore. Here, let me see if I can fit the champagne in. You get the bags, Bob. I'll finish this." As she packed their lunch, Karin explained that she'd recently found out she could be held liable for an accident involving a tourist who had just been served alcohol by her.

"Oh, my! Just for one glass of champagne?" exclaimed Meg. "I suppose you were told by that nice efficient Mr. Connors."

"No!" Karin snapped. "I was told by that nice Mr. Peterson and that most efficient Ms. Wentworth." At Meg's sharp look, she blushed and quickly added, "Just one of the pertinent tidbits I learned at my first management meeting. It was really a very valuable personal consultation with his two top executives."

"Oh?" Meg looked surprised. "I thought Mr. Connors himself would—"

"Mr. Connors is a very busy man. He owns the company, Meg, plus another one in Philadelphia, and I think he quite often goes back there. Anyway, except for one quick lunch, I've hardly had a glimpse of him since I joined."

Which was quite all right with her, she told herself. Blake Connors wasn't her reason for joining New Ventures. She swallowed, stifling the vague feeling of disappointment that plagued her, and smiled brightly at Meg. "There. All finished. I got everything in."

"So, let's get this show on the road," Bob muttered as he picked up the cooler. "I want an early start."

"And I have to get ready for tomorrow's trip," Karin said. "I need to stop by the complex before noon to pick up muffins from Dolly and the passenger list from the office—along with, mind you, advance deposits." She gave a satisfied smirk and winked at Meg. "Another valuable tidbit. This way, I don't lose money on last-minute dropouts. You're right, Bob. It was smart to join."

AS SHE DROVE to the complex, the feeling persisted. "A feeling of sadness and longing,/ that is not akin to pain,/ and resembles sorrow only/ as the mist resembles rain." She couldn't remember when she'd first read those lines of Longfellow's, but never had she understood them so well. And why, for heaven's sake, was she being so foolishly sentimental over a man she'd known for only a few short weeks!

Because no man had ever appealed to her the way he did. No man had ever kissed her the way he had, made her feel so...so wonderful. And then what? He'd become distant, withdrawn. He hadn't asked her for another date. Well, he'd taken her to lunch that time he ran into her at the complex, but even then he'd been, well, distant. Polite and interested, but only in her business. "How are you doing? Are you getting everything you need from us?" It seemed to her that he emphasized the impersonal "us" as if to make her understand that he was backing off from any personal involvement with her. And it was obvious that K. Palmer Tours had been delegated to Vickie Wentworth's jurisdiction.

Karin swallowed. Why should she resent that? Vickie was competent and had made several constructive suggestions. Oh, yes, the ever-efficient Ms. Wentworth seemed to be indispensable to New Ventures, handling several accounts, as well as overseeing the day-to-day operation of the business. And, judging by the glimpses Karin had caught of the two of them with their heads close together, she must be personally indispensable to Blake Connors, too!

Karin Palmer, you're jealous!

She had to be honest with herself. At first she'd thought . . . Yes, it did seem that he was attracted to her. But now . . . Her fingers tightened on the wheel and she flushed with embarrassment. Had he been turned off that night at the pool when she'd acted so unsophisticated? Scared out of her wits, overwhelmed by the strange new emotion that had gripped her?

So be grateful, Karin Palmer! Be glad he's backed off! You could become putty in that man's hands—probably like every other woman he encounters. She wondered about his relationship with Vickie Wentworth, then forced herself to stop.

Deliberately she focused her rebellious mind away from Blake Connors. She thought about *My Fair Lady,* an excellent musical; she'd enjoyed it so much at the Music Circus last night with Richard. Richard. Was it fair to continue going out with him? It had been all right when it was fun and games—but now? He seemed to be getting serious, which concerned her, since she knew he could never be more than a friend to her. Perhaps she should tell him again . . .

But now she was turning into the complex, and her thoughts reverted to tomorrow's trip and the necessary preparations. When she entered the building, she immediately boarded the elevator for the third floor, not even glancing toward Blake's office. Ruth had the passenger list and deposits all ready for her, and Karin drove to the other building looking forward to her usual pleasant coffee break with Dolly.

However, no sooner had Dolly filled their mugs than Jane burst in, looking like a thundercloud.

"Do you know what that snake has done?" she exclaimed.

"Snake?" asked Dolly.

"That lousy conniving Blake Connors," Jane answered, and Karin gasped. Jane had been loudest of all in her praise of Blake. Now she was singing a very different tune as she went on to explain how Connors had squashed some big job her fiancé had expected to get. "Jack had already talked to someone in contracts who said the City Library job was practically in his lap. And today he finds his bid has been eliminated. Jack says he knows it was Connors, that son of a you-know-what, who badmouthed him out of the deal."

"Oh, Jane, be reasonable," Dolly protested. "Mr. Connors isn't even on the planning commission or with the city in any capacity. How could he...?"

"Uh-huh. But you can't tell me he didn't use his very considerable influence to get back at Jack."

"But I don't understand." Karin put down her coffee mug and said in puzzled concern, "I should think Mr. Connors would be on his side."

"Oh, Mr. Blake Connors blows hot and cold."

Karin felt herself blush. How well she knew this! But surely in business... "He seems to be fair," she said, feeling compelled to defend him. "And always supportive."

"If everything's going great and he's getting a big slice of the pie. You'd better just watch your step, Karin. Ask Dolly what he did to Jack. I've got to get back to my shop.'' Jane flounced out, and Karin turned a puzzled face to Dolly.

Dolly shrugged. ''I don't know what happened. It seems Jack was getting some pretty big jobs, and New Ventures wanted a bigger percentage, and Jack got mad and pulled out. And now he thinks they're getting back at him.''

''I don't believe it!'' Karin said hotly.

''Well, it's all I can do to keep up with my own business,'' Dolly said, shrugging. ''But I must say, I've always received a square deal here.''

''So have I,'' Karin agreed. ''Of course, I've only been here a short time, but I don't think Blake Connors is either greedy or vindictive.''

''No.'' Dolly looked thoughtful. ''But he is ambitious. And so is Jack Austin. And with the kind of money they're talking about, there's a lot of wheeling and dealing that goes on. I'm not sure I'd want to get tangled up in that kind of competition.'' She sighed. ''Mr. Connors was asking me again about sending out samples to a grocery chain. The truth is, Karin, I don't think I want to get any bigger than I am.''

''Oh?''

''I'm a good cook. Good enough to know that with quantity you can sometimes lose quality.''

''I suppose that's true.'' The main reason Karin used Dolly's goods was that they truly tasted home-baked.

''Sometimes,'' mused Dolly, ''I wish I was back in my small catering business working out of my own kitchen.''

''But you're doing so well here! You can't mean that,'' Karin said.

Dolly laughed. ''No. I do feel more secure. I don't have to worry about college fees for Keith anymore. But on the other hand . . .'' She sighed deeply. ''It's been a bad day.

I just had a big argument with Keith.'' She explained that Keith wanted to go home to join some of his friends at the park and play basketball, but she had to work late and, anyway, didn't much want him to go. "He says I don't trust him, but it's not that. It's other people ... So much goes on these days and I worry. I liked it better when I could look out my window at him and his friends tossing baskets in my driveway.'' She stood to clear away the coffee mugs. "But I know I can't keep him cooped up. He's a good boy and really great about helping me.'' She sighed again. "I finally told him he could go home on the bus as soon as he finishes packing those tarts. You know how boys are about sports.''

"I do know and I'm glad you're letting him go,'' Karin said. "And he won't have to take the bus. I'll drop him by your house.''

Later, as Karin departed with Keith, Dolly called anxiously after her son, "Be back from the park by six. There's chili you can warm for dinner, but make yourself a salad. And don't have any of your friends over till I get there.''

"Okay, Mom. Sure. Okay,'' came the jubilant if rather absentminded responses to all the admonitions.

It must be hard being a single mother, Karin thought, as a grinning Keith climbed into the front seat beside her. Dolly was too protective. *Just as I would be,* she admitted, *if I had a son like Keith—so handsome, healthy, good-natured and just on the brink of manhood. It's a big responsibility.*

"So you're a basketball player?'' she asked.

"Aw, man, no. I just, you know, play. Like, I'll never be a Michael Jordan.''

She shot him a quick glance. "You sound disappointed.''

"Aw, man, yeah. Those guys make biiig bucks! And they get shoes and T-shirts named after them—stuff like that."

"Well, to each his own. Maybe you'll become rich and famous one day doing what *you* do best."

"Aw, man. I'm not all that good at baseball, either. And Mom says I can't sign up for football next year. She says her heart can't take it anymore."

Karin stifled a smile. "I wasn't thinking of sports. Maybe what Michael Jordan does with a basketball you can do with a pencil."

"Huh?"

"You like to draw, don't you?"

"Draw?" He sounded surprised.

"Those sketches on the table back at your mom's bakery—weren't they yours?"

"Oh, yeah, them. Aw, man! I just kinda, you know, fool around."

"Pretty good fooling around," Karin said. "I liked those drawings of a dog. Your dog?"

"Cookie? Yeah." Keith gave a little chuckle. "He's funny."

"Do you have any more sketches?"

"Of Cookie? Oh, yeah. Lots."

"Really? I'd like to see them," she said. Every time she'd visited with Dolly at her complex, she'd studied Keith's drawings; there were always some of them lying about. She thought the boy had real talent. "Do you have time for me to take a look?" she asked, turning into his driveway.

"Uh...sure. I mean, if you want to. The guys aren't picking me up until two." He slanted her a doubtful, al-most apologetic glance as he led her into the neat frame house. "They're not all that great. I just, like, mess

DOUBLE YOUR ACTION PLAY...

"ROLL A DOUBLE!"

Peel off label & place inside

**CLAIM UP TO 4 BOOKS
PLUS A LOVELY
"KEY TO YOUR HEART"
PENDANT NECKLACE**

ABSOLUTELY FREE!

SEE INSIDE...

NO RISK, NO OBLIGATION TO BUY...NOW OR EVER!

GUARANTEED

PLAY "ROLL A DOUBLE" AND GET AS MANY AS FIVE FREE GIFTS!

HERE'S HOW TO PLAY:

1. Peel off label from front cover. Place it in space provided at right. With a coin, carefully scratch off the silver dice. This makes you eligible to receive two or more free books, and possibly another gift, depending on what is revealed beneath the scratch-off area.

2. You'll receive brand-new Harlequin Romance® novels. When you return this card, we'll rush you the books and gift you qualify for ABSOLUTELY FREE!

3. Then, if we don't hear from you, every month we'll send you 6 additional novels to read and enjoy months before they arrive in stores. You can return them and owe nothing, but if you decide to keep them, you'll pay only $2.49* per book— a saving of 40¢ each off the cover price—plus only 69¢ delivery for the entire shipment.

4. When you subscribe to the Harlequin Reader Service®, you'll also get our subscribers'-only newsletter, as well as additional free gifts from time to time.

5. You must be completely satisfied. You may cancel at any time simply by sending us a note or a shipping statement marked "cancel" or by returning any shipment to us at our expense.

The Austrian crystal sparkles like a diamond! And it's carefully set in a romantic "Key to Your Heart" pendant on a generous 18" gold-tone chain. The entire necklace is yours free as added thanks for giving our Reader Service a try!

HARLEQUIN "NO RISK" GUARANTEE

- You're not required to buy a single book—ever!
- You must be completely satisfied or you may cancel at any time simply by sending us a note or shipping statement marked "cancel" or by returning any shipment to us at our cost. Either way, you will receive no more books; you'll have no obligation to buy.
- The free books and gift you claimed on this "Roll A Double" offer remain yours to keep no matter what you decide.

DETACH AND MAIL CARD TODAY!

Business Reply Mail

No Postage Stamp Necessary if Mailed in Canada

Postage will be paid by

HARLEQUIN READER SERVICE
PO BOX 609
FORT ERIE, ONT.
L2A 9Z9

Canada Post
Postes Canada
125

around." They were greeted by frantic barking, and Keith went immediately to the sliding glass doors at the back to admit the little wire-haired terrier.

"Amazing," she said as she watched Keith lovingly pet the exuberant dog. "You caught him exactly."

Keith gave a sheepish grin and murmured an embarrassed thanks. He disappeared for a moment, then came back, and with an anxious expression, handed her a folder containing several sketches of the dog in various poses. "Uh...guess I better feed Cookie," he said, and seemed glad to withdraw to the kitchen. Karin spread the drawings on the dining table and stared at the precise graceful lines. The boy was a natural.

"These are very good," she told Keith when he returned.

"Uh, thanks."

"These expressions are almost human. That's the real difference between a photograph and a painting." She had a sudden thought. "Did you ever try portraits?"

For an instant he looked as if he'd been caught with his hand in the cookie jar, and he hesitated before he said, "Not exactly."

"What do you mean, not exactly?"

"Aw, man! They're, you know, funny. Mom says I might be crucified if I was to show them around."

"Oh? You mean they're caricatures?" When he nodded, she said, "I'd really like to see them." But it took quite a bit of persuading before he decided that since he hadn't done any of her, it would be all right to let her have a look.

"Here's one I did of Jane," he said when he finally brought them out.

It was Jane all right, but very exaggerated—eyes wide, false lashes fluttering, in a typical pose calculated to show the diamond on her finger. Another of Dolly with flour on her nose and an exaggeratedly smug smile on her face as she displayed one of her pies.

"And who's this?" Karin asked once she'd stopped laughing. She pointed to a sketch of a man who was crouching and had the menacing look of a bulldog.

"That's the football coach." Keith, who had been shifting uncomfortably from one foot to the other, managed an embarrassed grin.

Karin studied the caricatures, utterly astonished. They were clever, even professional. Suddenly she turned back to Keith. "How would you like to do a logo for me?"

"What's that?"

"It's a symbol that identifies an enterprise or business. It usually appears on a letterhead, or circulars sent out by that business," she explained. "I'd like a striking picture that would make people immediately think "art" and "tour.""

He stared at her, looking rather stupefied. "And you want me to do one? Aw, man," he protested, "I'm not that good. Like I said I just, you know, mess around."

She shook her head. The boy had the touch of genius and didn't know it. She gestured toward his drawings. "You mean you don't know how good these are? Don't your teachers say anything to you?"

"Are you kidding?" He looked shocked. "Coach would nail me! And I sure couldn't show that one of the principal to my teachers. Man!"

"Oh, Keith! Keith!" Karin laughed and impulsively shook his arm. "Well, I'll tell you how good you are. I'll pay you a hundred dollars if you do my logo."

"Man! A hundred dollars!" Keith, obviously startled by the mention of such a sum, stood awkwardly, rubbing his hands on his jeans, eyes wide. "Aw, man, I couldn't. I wouldn't know where to start."

"Oh, just do something making me look silly. Maybe struggling with an easel and trying to board a bus."

"You mean, like funny?"

"The funnier the better!"

"I... Look, I could try, but—" he hesitated "—and look, it's okay if you don't... I mean, you might not like it. And, anyway, you wouldn't have to pay me anything."

Karin was examining the drawings again, but now she turned back to Keith. "Listen, Keith, a man is worthy of his hire, and it's a lucky man who can make money doing what he enjoys. Oh, I'll pay you." She laughed. "And I'll be getting off cheap before you become rich and famous!"

"Me?" Keith looked bewildered.

"Have you ever heard of Charles Schulz?"

"Who's he?"

"Just one of the wealthiest cartoonists in the country. You've read *Peanuts*, haven't you?"

"Oh, yeah. That guy."

"And I suppose you've heard of Walt Disney?" When he nodded, an awed look on his face, she said. "He liked to fool around with a pencil, too, and one day he just happened to doodle a silly cartoon of a mouse. And you know what came out of that! Now, do you have time before your friends get here? We could sit down for a few minutes and talk about what I want."

"You've got the right idea," she said a half hour later. "I think I'll leave it with you. Call me when you're ready."

"Yeah, man." Keith was so busy sketching he didn't look up as Karin, smiling, let herself out.

CHAPTER EIGHT

BLAKE HAD DECIDED not to see Karin Palmer again, at least not privately.

Of course she attracted him, had always attracted him. But then, so had many other women with whom he'd enjoyed... How had she put it? Oh, yes, pleasant interludes. And, yes, it was with a pleasant interlude in mind that he'd sought Karin out. He was in the midst of the pursuit when he'd sensed Karin might become more than that. Much more. It wasn't the kiss, though Lord knew that was powerful enough, ripe with the promises of erotic pleasures. No. It was the promise of an intimacy far beyond the physical that scared him. Once, a long time ago, he'd shared that kind of intimacy—and been deeply hurt when he lost it.

Karin had been the one to retreat, frightened, he knew, by the same consuming passion that had gripped him. But her retreat had given him time to gain control of himself and back off. Since that night, he'd been careful to avoid any more personal contact.

Then he happened to bump into her. It was just the other day, and she'd been coming out of the elevator with Mrs. Spencer's boy. She'd looked so radiantly enthusiastic, smiled that captivating smile, ambushed his whole attention with her zest and eagerness...

''Look! Just look at these!'' She rushed toward him, her dimples dancing, eyes glowing, and thrust a couple of papers into his hand. "Keith just did these graphics on the computer upstairs. Isn't he great? He made several drawings for me. They were all so good I couldn't decide. So he put my two favorites on the computer and I still can't decide. Which one do you like?"

He loved seeing her this way, so animated, so refreshingly alive. But that was Karin, always charmingly eager and intent on whatever she was doing—directing a tour group, involved in that messy canning, cavorting in a swimming pool. Or... He studied the enchanting curve of her lips, remembering.

"Which one do you like?" she prompted.

"Oh. Hmm." He forced his gaze away from her to the papers in his hand. Two drawings. One a caricature of her loaded with easel and paintbrush, the other an enlarged face of her leaning out of a bus and motioning with a paintbrush. "And this is for...?"

"A logo for me. For my cards, brochures, stationery and so on."

"Oh." He examined the two drawings. Very well done. Clever and humorous. But as a come-on for serious art lovers? He doubted this was the right approach.

"Of course, on my cards it would be so tiny it might not show up. But on the brochures it would really be an eye-catcher. I think I lean toward this one," she said, pointing to the one of her gesturing from the bus. "What do you think?"

He looked again at Karin, so exuberant, then at the silent wide-eyed boy beside her.

"These are both excellent," he said decisively. "But why don't you come into my office and we'll talk this over." He didn't want to deflate the boy's ego or Karin's enthusiasm, but this simply wasn't the type of logo to attract her special clientele. Once in his office, with Karin and Keith seated before him, he leaned against his desk and tried to tactfully explain.

"It's uncanny," he said, "how much people are affected by little things. And artists are especially sensitive. Here—" he touched the drawings "—it's as if you're making fun of their very serious interest."

"Oh." Karin looked a little dubious. "I hadn't thought..." She glanced at Keith. The boy seemed positively crushed, and she spoke again quickly as if to reassure him. "I told him to make it funny."

Yes, she would, Blake thought. She was that kind of person, living life with a light touch, finding a delightful sense of joy in everything she did. He turned to Keith, who now seemed quite unsure.

"You delivered just what she ordered," he said to the boy. "These are excellent. You have a rare talent. But—" Blake now turned to Karin "—the object is to promote your business. You have to consider the sensitivities of your potential customers, figure out what will appeal to them."

Her expression was a little daunted, but she seemed to get his point. "I know what you mean. But I do want a picture—one that makes a statement. And I want Keith to do it."

"Aw, man." Keith shifted uncomfortably in his chair. "It's okay. Like I told you, if you didn't like it—"

"But I do like it," Karin insisted. "It's just that Mr. Connors thinks it wouldn't work. We'll have to think of something else. A drawing that would get the same idea across, but wouldn't poke fun, see?"

"Aw, man." Keith shook his head doubtfully.

"You can do it," Blake said.

"I don't... You know, I just draw, like, funny."

Blake laughed. "Believe me, son, anybody who can draw humor can draw anything. You can do it. Here, pull your chairs up," he said as he began to clear his desk. "Let's toss around a few ideas."

It was an invigorating half hour. There were some contentious moments, with Blake trying to match his conservative business nature to Karin's free-spirited and somewhat childlike approach. Keith watched as they argued, focusing on one and then the other, but remaining silent and apart until Karin protested.

"Come on, Keith," she urged. "You're the artist and you had all those ideas before."

"Aw, man," he demurred.

"Well, start sketching, anyway." Blake pushed a pad toward him. "Karin wants the bus in, but I think..." They began to pour out different ideas, and it was amazing how quickly and skillfully Keith could sketch each concept. The boy was good, Blake thought. He must speak to Mrs. Spencer. This talent should be encouraged and developed.

It was Keith who finally came up with a workable solution.

"Well, it's like you..." He paused, rubbing his hand on his jeans. "You know, like you want to get in the art and travel both," he said hesitantly. "Look, maybe if we leave out the bus—and you," he added apologetically to Karin, "and do this... It's kinda simple, but..." They watched as he sketched a rough draft of a map of California, a paintbrush poised over it. "And colors like from here and here... you know, going to different places."

"Great!" Karin cried, her face beaming. "That's it!"

"I agree," said Blake. "You've caught the idea exactly, Keith. It's perfect."

"Aw, man," was all Keith said, but his wide grin showed how he basked in Blake's approval.

"I would like one change, though," Blake added. "An easy one. Change California to a globe of the world."

"Oh, sure." Karin looked up, smiling, ready to share the joke. Then, "You're not kidding!" she exclaimed.

"Of course not. You don't want to limit yourself." But even as he said it, he remembered Vickie's sarcastic "trips to the Louvre in Paris and perhaps a few to Amsterdam." Well, why the hell not, he thought, watching Karin's dubious expression change to one of glowing anticipation.

"I suppose there's no limit to what a businessperson can accomplish once he or she is part of New Ventures," she said. "Thank you. For your grand ideas and for the time. I know how busy you are," she said as she and Keith departed.

Blake stared at his closed office door, feeling a little guilty. Here he was, encouraging her to expand but hardly lifting a finger to help her do it. True, he took no part in the everyday operations of his tenants. The management meetings and such were under the jurisdiction of Pete, Vickie and a couple of other trained staff people. But he always took an interest and checked on each tenant's progress. He must not neglect K. Palmer Tours, he thought as he flicked on his intercom.

"Let me have the Palmer Tours' account," he said to Vickie.

She looked at him with surprise when she brought it in, murmuring, "She hasn't been with us quite two months." He merely nodded and Vickie quietly withdrew.

He thumbed through the pages. Just as he suspected, she was barely making it. So excited about that damn logo, but it would take more than a logo to get her off the ground. And probably more than art. He tapped a finger on his desk, absently keeping time with the chant reverberating in his mind, the old well-proven remedy—find a need and fill it. He was irritated when Vickie interrupted to remind him of his lunch date with Bill Snowden.

But it was Snowden who supplied the need. Snowden had been one of Blake's first tenants when he opened New Ventures in Philadelphia, and he'd become spectacularly successful. His Philadelphia plant, which manufactured gourmet-cooking utensils, had expanded rapidly, and he was in town laying the groundwork for the opening of his new Sacramento plant.

"I'm concerned about my employees," he told Blake, "especially some of the key personnel I'd like to move from my Philly plant—dyed-in-the-wool Easterners who want no part of the West Coast."

"You need to sponsor a few relocation tours to lure them here," Blake said. "In fact . . . I have just the person to handle them for you." Snowden enthusiastically agreed to this plan.

Later, on the point of departing for a board meeting in New York and a visit to his New Ventures office in Philadelphia, Blake instructed Vickie to have Karin begin preparations for the project immediately.

He felt quite excited about this. It would be a very lucrative sideline for Karin. He knew of other companies moving into the fast-growing Sacramento area who could also use these services. Understandably, when he returned a week later, he was shocked and rather annoyed when Vickie informed him that Karin had turned down the project.

"What the hell do you mean, she turned it down?" he almost shouted.

"Just that. She said it wasn't in her line." Vickie studied her nails before lifting innocent eyes to his. "Shall I suggest Snowden find another source?"

"No!" He did shout now and didn't bother to lower his voice when he added, "I'll talk to Snowden. No, damn it, I'll talk to Karin. Not her line! She's in the tour business, isn't she? And the point is to make it pay. Didn't you explain that to her?"

Vickie shrugged. "You know our policy, Blake. We only advise. We don't interfere." Again she shrugged. "If she wants to run a roving art gallery..."

But her words were lost on Blake who slammed into his office, grabbed his phone and dialed. Somebody had better interfere!

The phone was answered by her zany aunt. "Oh, Mr. Connors! How nice to hear from you. I was just asking Karin if you— What? Oh, no, Karin isn't here. She took a group of students from the college up to the Mendocino Art Center to hear Jacoby Sands... Sands. You know, the political cartoonist. Why, he can show you the monkey inside a phony politician with just a few strokes of his pen. Very clever, but not really my thing. I much prefer pretty to clever and that's why I stick to nature. Nature can also make a statement, you know— What? Oh, no. Karin won't be back for several days— What? They're staying over at Hill House. Such a lovely place, so full of history. And they'll probably go to the Mendocino Hotel for that Sunday-morning brunch... Silly— so much food and so confusing. One never knows whether to eat breakfast, lunch or dinner, and it's so difficult to separate what's really nutritious from— What? Oh. Oh, yes, I see. Well, shall I tell Karin you— Oh, well, goodbye."

He returned the phone to its cradle, rubbing his ear. Damn! Karin wouldn't be back for several days, and she needed to get on top of this in a hurry if she was to get Snowden's business.

He looked down at the appointment schedule Vickie had handed him. Full. But this was Friday. If he canceled tomorrow's golf...

IT WAS A LITTLE before noon on Saturday when he reached the narrow rocky road that twisted down to the little village of Mendocino. He had no trouble locating the Hill House Inn, a charming Victorian-style structure close to the center of town. He was lucky, the desk clerk informed him, to get the last available room. Karin, however, was not in.

"She's probably with her tour group at the Mendocino Art Center," the man said, then pointed the way. "It's only a short walk."

As Blake strolled among the crowd of people milling about the art galleries and restaurants, he sensed a feeling of complacency and general camaraderie. He thought of his one-sided conversation with Karin's loquacious aunt. He had to agree that the town was lovely, a perfect setting for an arts weekend. So full of history, indeed, with its quaint streets and carefully restored old houses, r. nging from simple saltboxes to Victorian showplaces. A real coastal town, he thought, as the fresh sea air filled his lungs.

The hotel clerk had told him that the sprawling Art Center consisted of several buildings, including a theater, an art gallery and three studios, as well as housing for students. He'd expected to have to search among them for Karin's group, but he was lucky. Almost as soon as he entered the spacious grounds he spotted Keith among a group of people emerging from one of the larger buildings. So Karin was making a protégé of the talented boy. Yes, she would, he thought, smiling to himself.

"Keith!" he called.

"Mr. Connors! I didn't know you were here. Aw, man! it was awesome!" Keith's eyes were alight with amazement. Clearly he was too overcome by the demonstration he'd just witnessed to be surprised at Blake's presence. "Awesome," he repeated.

Blake smiled. "That good, huh? I'm glad you got the chance to see him." He glanced over Keith's shoulder, searching the crowds. "Where's Karin?" he asked.

"Huh? Oh. She went to do some sketching. Says she's not into this kinda stuff. But, man! She shoulda seen Sands." Keith dismissed Karin with a shrug, and his usual shyness disappeared as he tried to share his interest in Sands's kind of art. "You know, he goes like this!" Keith gestured in the air, drawing quick lines with one finger. "And like this!" Another lightning stroke. His eyes squinted with astonishment. "Major speed! And then he's all done—the whole picture!"

Though he was frustrated at not finding Karin, Blake could not help being amused and pleased by the teenager's show of enthusiasm. "I take it you were impressed," he said.

"Aw, man! You saw how he—"

"No, I didn't," Blake cut in. "I just walked over. I wasn't there."

"Oh."

"But I know he's good. I've seen his work."

"Oh, yeah. I guess most people know that stuff." Something in his tone caught Blake's full attention. He glanced at the crumpled folder under Keith's arm.

"Did he see samples of your work?"

"Aw, man."

Funny, Blake thought, how that one phrase always conveyed Keith's highs and lows. That last was definitely a low. But surely Sands recognized Keith's talent. Then it occurred to him that he hadn't seen much of the boy's work himself.

"Come over here and let me take a look at what you showed him," he said, moving to a bench under a nearby spreading oak.

When they were seated Keith opened the folder and displayed his sketches. "That's my principal and that's the coach," he explained. "Karin said to be sure to show him those, and I thought, you know, like it was okay 'cause Mr. Sands didn't know them."

"And?" These were excellent. Surely the man could see that.

"He said that was the problem. Nobody would know them. Not, you know, like they'd recognize pictures of the president or somebody big. It's like these kinds of pictures have to be universal or something."

Ah, yes. Sands had a point, Blake thought.

"Still, these are very well done. Didn't he say anything about your technique?" Or was Sands a pompous jerk who—

"Oh, yeah. He said I had...a flair for this kinda thing," Keith said, brightening. "And he really liked these drawings of Cookie, my dog."

Blake thumbed through the sketches, becoming more and more impressed.

"Hey, Keith!" One of a group of boys descending the steps of the studio called to him. "We're going for burgers. Wanna come?"

"Oh, sure," Keith answered, glancing at Blake.

"Go ahead. Only, do you mind if I hold on to these? Just for a while."

"Oh, sure. I mean, it's okay," Keith said, looking a little puzzled. "You can have 'em if you want."

Blake lifted a hand. "Careful, Keith! Don't toss away your rights so casually." He touched the folder containing the drawings. "You never know when they might become universally recognizable—and therefore commercially feasible."

"Huh?"

Blake grinned. "Never mind. Go on with your friends. I'll be in touch." But as the boys started off, he called to them, "Just a minute, please. Do any of you know which way Karin went?"

"Oh, sure," one of them answered. "She's on the beach just down from the headlands. Across from the Mendocino Hotel. Said she wanted to do some sketching."

THE ROCK WAS LARGE and jutted from the edge of the beach out into the sea. It was relatively flat and afforded an excellent view of her surroundings. Karin håd climbed up and now sat alone, her paint box open beside her. Almost directly below her, two children, under the watchful eyes of their mother, dashed in and out of the cold water, but their delighted cries hardly penetrated her consciousness. She was only dimly aware of the other people who made the precarious descent down the cliffs or strolled along the beach. On each of her tours, especially the longer ones, she always tried to arrange a period of "on your own" time. A period of free time to do as you chose—browse among the shops, ramble through the countryside or stand as long as you liked before some museum masterpiece. A bonus for herself, as well as her tourists, Karin thought. Another perk of being a tour guide. Despite the assistance of New Ventures, she had to admit she wasn't making much money, not nearly as much as she'd received as a typist for Water Resources. But the perks made the difference. What other job offered free travel and free time to enjoy such places as this! Time to sit quietly, to absorb and drink in the beauty!

To capture it?

She drew in a deep breath as her gaze wandered along the craggy headlands that jutted out into the sea and focused on the turbulent waterfall gushing from a huge tunnel, the most spectacular of the famous blowholes cut by the sea through the massive coastal rocks. It was aptly named the Devil's Punch Bowl, Karin thought, studying the giant geyser as it roared and spurted high into the air. But it was too beautiful to be sinister. She watched the frothy white dance of the spray above the great sheet of water, a mass of shimmering bottle-green in the glow of the midday sun. If only she could catch the movement, the hues...

She looked down at the watercolor she'd started on sketching paper carefully taped to a flat board. She looked again at the waterfall, then back to her painting, shook her head and sighed. Okay, so she wasn't the world's greatest artist. Which was why she always used one-hundred-percent erasable rag paper. She dipped her sponge in water, squeezed and gently scrubbed the paper clean. Doggedly she began again, carefully scrutinizing the waterfall as she mixed her colors.

Half an hour later she put down her paintbrush and took a shiny red apple from her tote bag. Munching on the apple, she sat back to compare her finished painting with the real thing. Not perfect, but not bad. Was the shade of green just a trifle too—?

"Now that's pretty darn good!" Startled, she turned to see Blake Connors sitting back on his heels, staring at her sketch. For a moment she was filled with a sensation of such sheer pleasure that all other reactions, even surprise, were blotted out. He wasn't looking at her, but was studying her watercolor with an intensity that made her uncomfortable. "I didn't know you were an artist yourself."

"No. Well, not really. I just . . . dabble a little." Darn! She sounded like Keith. And she couldn't shift her gaze from Blake's face. What was he doing here and why was her heart thudding so wildly? Her breath caught as his fingers encircled her wrist to pull her hand toward his mouth.

"The least you can do is share," he said, taking a hefty bite of her apple, "since you made me miss lunch."

"Me? I made you . . ." Her voice trailed off when she felt his thumb gently caressing her wrist as he again drew the apple to his mouth.

"Hmm. Not quite as sweet as pineapple," he mused, his voice low and loaded with a sensual significance that made her body throb with hot waves of pleasure. She could almost taste the pungent sweetness of the pineapple, almost feel his lips on hers—possessing, demanding, delighting. As if suddenly regretting the implied intimacy, he released her hand and settled himself quite apart from her.

She tried to get a firm grip on her emotions, but there was a catch in her voice. "I'm surprised. I mean, what are you doing here?"

"Looking for you."

"For me?" He'd come all this way just to see her?

He nodded. "No easy task. I expected to find you at the Art Center with your group."

"Oh, no," she answered vaguely, wondering why this man, who'd been avoiding her for weeks, had come so far to see her. "Portraits and caricatures aren't really my line."

"So I see." He glanced at her painting again. "You prefer pretty to clever?"

"What?"

"And do you contend that nature also makes a statement?"

"A statement?" He seemed highly amused and she tried to fathom his meaning.

"As Sands does with his caricatures of our key political figures."

"Oh. Well, I hadn't thought about it, but..." His deep blue eyes seemed to be laughing at her and she felt defensive. "Well, yes," she said rather defiantly. "Nature does make a statement."

"Oh?"

"Yes." She stuck the apple core into a plastic bag, along with her discarded papers, dusted her hands and said decisively, "How could you look at all this—" her gesture took in their surroundings "—and not recognize the inevitability of—" she searched for the right word "—nature...life...God?"

He gave her an intent look. "You mean, 'God's in his heaven and all's right with the world'?"

"Well, something like that," she said earnestly. "You see a small sign of the...divine order, I guess, that controls our world and it does give you a feeling of peace. Whatever happens, the earth will still turn, the sun still rise and set, the seas, the sand, all the beauty, will remain." Darn! She must sound like a dizzy Pollyanna. She lowered her eyes and couldn't look at him.

"That's quite a statement." He sounded thoughtful and she glanced at him under her lashes. He had been gazing at the waterfall, but now he picked up her sketch and examined it. She wished he wouldn't. "And this is what you portray? This sense of inevitable order—or whatever you want to call it?"

"Yes, perhaps. But then again, no. Yes, because we all try. And no, since we're merely human. To really portray this is beyond us."

"But you try."

"I do indeed," she said reflectively. "Each component of this seascape provides a different color and emotion, a different shape..." She stopped, embarrassed. Then she gave a little shrug and spoke softly. "It defies imitation."

"I think, Karin Palmer, that I'm finding hidden depths in you."

Again she glanced at him. Was he mocking her? But as she saw the tender sincerity in his eyes, she felt a warm glow steal through her.

They sat together a long while, conversing casually about Mendocino and how the little village had managed to retain its old-world charm, despite the influx of crowds and moviemakers. Even the long silences, broken only by the cry of gulls and the rush of waves against the rocks, seemed companionable. Karin felt happy, peaceful, and even forgot to wonder why he had come.

When he said quite casually, "Tell me, Karin, how do you like being a part of New Ventures?" her answer came spontaneously, instantly.

"Oh, I love it! It's made everything so much easier. And it's given me so much more free time."

His mouth twisted wryly. "I don't think that's the main objective."

"No, of course not." She flushed, remembering what Jane had said more than once. *Sure, Connors comes across as easygoing, tolerant. But you'd better not forget, he's always got his eye on the dollar signs.* Had they checked her balance sheets already and found she wasn't measuring up?

"I've been looking over your records," he said, confirming her fears, "and your profits seem to be slipping. Your connection with New Ventures has been counter-productive to our major purpose, which is to make money for you."

"Oh, no. You're not..." But the words couldn't get past the apprehensive lump in her throat. She was being ridiculous. Surely he wouldn't travel all this way just to tell her she was being dropped. Still, she felt a prickle of fear.

CHAPTER NINE

"I'VE BEEN GOING OVER your records with Vickie."

Karin stiffened, the old resentment flaring. She had explained to Meg and Bob that Blake was a busy man, had pretended not to resent his turning her account over to Vickie. As if to make it clear that their relationship was only a business one. He hadn't come near her since the night at the swimming pool. Except for that one quick lunch, more business than pleasure, and that day with Keith.

"...and I can't understand why," he was saying, looking rather irked. Karin blinked, utterly confused, so lost had she been in her own thoughts. But at his next words her head jerked up. "The Snowden job could bring your balance sheet into some kind of order. Didn't you say something once about not looking a gift horse in the mouth?"

"And wasn't it you who told me I should?" Now she was really angry. There had been something so condescending about Vickie's manner when she'd said, "We've decided to let you handle Snowden's relocation tours." The whole idea had made Karin shudder. "Subdivisions and shopping centers are not in my line," she'd said then, and she said it again now.

"You seem to be pretty definite about what's in your line." His terse tone increased her irritation.

"I'm not ashamed. My line is art—museums, lessons, sketching tours and so on. The kind of things I enjoy."

"Oh?" He gave her a skeptical look. "The day I met you I believe you were on a gambling tour."

She tossed her head. "I told you I do that as a favor to Mrs. Jackson. Basically I'm a tour guide who specializes in—"

"Stop right there!" He held up a hand. "You are not a tour guide. You are an entrepreneur. You own a business."

"Okay, I own a business. So?"

"You don't run a business as a favor to anyone or exclusively for your own pleasure. The object is to make money."

"Oh, yes. Let's keep our eyes on the dollar sign!" Immediately she regretted the sarcasm. She shouldn't let Jane's gossip goad her into making judgments. Still, she couldn't help asking, "Do you consider money the only measure of success?"

"I think that's the usual standard of measurement."

"Well, yes, in a strictly commercial context."

He quirked an eyebrow. "That *is* what we're talking about, isn't it?"

"All right, I'll buy that. But..." She frowned. She wasn't exactly in the red, even though she was now leasing buses. And she'd managed to make payments on the repair of Mr. Turner's bus. "Look," she said, "I'm not getting rich in a hurry, but I'm making it."

"Just barely." He gave her an even look. "How much, for instance, are you clearing on this trip?"

"Well, a little." She almost choked on the lie. She wasn't so much as breaking even. "But this is a special trip. It's most unusual for a man like Sands to be in this vicinity. And these are college kids especially interested in this art form. They haven't got much money, you see and..." She hesitated, shrugged. "Well, I set my price so they could afford the trip."

He had watched her intently during this rapid discourse and now he shook his head. "Karin, Karin. You're running a business, not a charity."

"But some of these kids have real talent, and I didn't want them to miss this opportunity. I'll make it up."

"You're not a talent scout, either. And I don't see how you'll make it up. As I told you, I looked over your records. You're not making a living wage. I don't see how you manage your personal expenses, housing and..."

"I don't," she conceded, chuckling. "I'm house-sitting for Meg and Bob, an arrangement we all enjoy. And so—"

"Wait a minute!" he said with some exasperation. "I don't want to get into all that. My view is definitely that one should make the best of one's talent, resources and time. In that context, the records say you're slipping. I want to help you fix it. Now let's think in terms of resources." He rubbed his fist against his cheek and took a deep breath. "To tell you the truth, Karin, from the very first I had reservations about a tour company whose success is wholly dependent upon art interests."

"Oh? You never said so." Her tone was tart. "In fact, it was you who maintained that my logo should encompass the world!" He'd made her feel so confident that afternoon. And now... She felt betrayed.

"Yes. Because I didn't want you to limit your possibilities. You always have to think in terms of growth."

"Maybe some of us don't want to grow." She thought of Dolly.

"A business either grows or it stagnates—and eventually dies."

"And your idea is that I should spread out. Latch on to whatever comes my way—gambling, relocation and convention tours...whatever."

"My idea is that the first priority of any business is to remain solvent. To build up some reserves so you can expand in the realm of your choice. Right now, art in itself will not support you. The Snowden project, in my view, would provide you with the leeway to indulge in these artsy losers."

Artsy losers! That did it. She stood and stared down at him, her eyes flashing. "Look, I quit a well-paying job to do what matters to me! I didn't expect to make a lot of money. I like what I'm doing and I won't be derailed by this grow-grow-grow mania! There's more to life than that!"

He also stood, looking genuinely puzzled by her outburst. "Damn it, Karin! You act like I asked you to cut your throat, instead of showing you how to increase your profits. As long as you're a tenant of New Ventures it's my duty to—"

"You didn't need to come all this way to drop me. I quit!" she said, stomping her foot. But Karin's vehemence was lost in the wake of a big wave that crashed over the rock, sending her tumbling into Blake's arms. Both of them were brought to a startling awareness. While they'd been yelling at each other, the tide had changed. Soon their rock would be swallowed by the turbulent ocean, which even now completely surrounded them. Instinctively Karin broke away from Blake and retrieved her sketch just before it could be engulfed by another oncoming wave. Holding the sketch high, she reached for her paint box.

"Let the damn thing go!" Blake shouted as he grabbed her about the waist. "We've got to get the hell off this

thing!'' He took the painting from her, but the tote bag
and paint box swirled crazily away.

When they climbed down from the rock, the water almost reached her chest, and she felt the full force of the
pounding tide. For a few moments she panicked, fearing
they'd both be caught in the undertow and swept out to
sea. Choking and sputtering, she clung tightly to Blake
as he half dragged her through the ferocious swell. They
were drenched and breathing hard when they finally
clambered up a small plateau, well above the rising tide.
Karin sank to the ground and gazed down at the beach,
now a part of the sea that swelled and gushed below
them.

"Well, Karin," said Blake, "nature just made one hell
of a statement. In fact, save for me, it might have been
the last heard by you."

"Hardly that." Karin felt tense and still a little frightened. "I'm a pretty good swimmer," she retorted, irked
by his grin.

"Ah, but you were about to be swept away to save your
art, which," he added, laughing as he laid the painting on
the ground beside her, "has remained safe and dry, again
thanks to me."

Karin, too cold and wet to feel grateful, only glanced
at the painting. "Mr. Connors," she said, drawing herself up. "None of this would have happened if you hadn't
distracted me. And you didn't notice the rising tide, either, since you were so busy telling me how to make
money, money, money!"

"Karin," he said softly, "that's because I'm on your
side. And now I'm more than ever convinced that your
penchant for art must be nurtured." Emptying water out
of one of her sneakers, Karin looked at him suspi-

ciously. He smiled at her. "The best way to do that is to make more money."

"And only you know the best way to do that!" she snapped, before almost choking on a violent sneeze.

"Right. That's my job. But I think we'd better dry out before debating the issue."

"No debate. You have your opinion and I have mine." But she tied her shoelace and they started back to Hill House Inn. They had almost reached it when she heard someone call her name. She turned to see Richard loping toward them, looking rather disheveled in swim trunks and T-shirt. A wet suit, goggles and flippers were flung over one arm.

"You should have come with me," he said. "I saw an octopus! Weird! All those tentacles curving around rocks and—"

"Aw, man!" Karin broke in, aping Keith so exactly that Blake burst into laughter. But she could tell by Richard's uncomprehending stare that he didn't share the joke. "Sorry I missed it," she added, trying not to shudder. "Richard, you remember Blake Connors, don't you? You two met at the house." She turned to remind Blake but was disconcerted by his expression of... what? Disapproval? Anger?

"Oh, sure," Richard said, shifting his goggles to the other arm and giving Blake a cheerful grin. "The incubator man. What are you doing in this area?"

"I was just about to ask you the same thing," said Blake. "Didn't know you were interested in art."

"Oh, not in art, just in a certain artist," Richard answered with a suggestive glance that made Karin flush. "So I just trail along, and while they gawk at pictures I go snorkeling."

"Here?" Blake asked him. "With this current and the rocks? Isn't that risky?"

"Oh, it's a bit rough, but I don't mind." They had entered the inn now, and Richard started down the hall toward his room. "So long. See you at dinner, Karin."

"Afraid not," said Blake.

"Oh?" Richard turned back.

"I'm taking Karin out to dinner tonight. We have some urgent business to discuss." His tone was pleasant but firm. "That's why I came down."

"Oh?" Richard said again, and looked questioningly at Karin.

"Um...yes," she said. She had been about to say this was the first she'd heard of dinner. But she sensed the tension. One minute they'd been pleasantly chatting about snorkeling and the next... "Mr. Connors has a project in mind that we need to talk about." She did owe him that much, she thought.

"Okay, see you in the morning." Richard gave a conciliatory wave and went on down the hall.

"Shall we have dinner here?" she asked Blake. "I have to see to—"

"That guy. What is he to you?"

"Richard? I already told you—just a friend," she replied, as surprised by the question as by the grim look on his face.

"Does he go along on all your tours?"

"Of course not," she said, laughing. "He does have a job." She stared at Blake. Could he possibly be jealous of Richard?

He seemed to become conscious of her scrutiny and dropped his eyes. "Six-thirty okay?" he asked. "I'll make reservations."

"Sure, if you want to eat here. My group—"

"Not here," he said as they entered the elevator.

"Then we'd better make it seven-thirty. I'll have to take in the dinner tickets and get my folks settled first."

Back in her room she dressed with care, glad she'd brought at least one decent dinner dress. It was a very simple off-white silk sheath with a low neck and long sleeves, and thank goodness, she'd brought the matching sandals. Blake's eyes lighted with appreciation as he helped her into the car.

"Thought we'd drive down the coast to a place I know," he said. "Just a small restaurant, but it has excellent seafood."

It was small, but quaint and very cozy in the glow of small captain's lamps on each table and a bright fire in the big stone fireplace.

"Oh, this is lovely!" Karin exclaimed. "I know it's the middle of August, but that fire does feel good."

"Yes," Blake agreed as he pulled out her chair. "Nights on the coast are pretty chilly."

Karin glanced around. The large room contained just six tables, and apart from theirs, only two were occupied, a middle-aged couple at one and two older women at the other. A young girl who looked like a high-school student acted as both hostess and waitress. Blake seemed to know her, and they chatted amiably as she poured their wine.

"Do you come here often?" Karin asked when the girl had moved to another table.

"Not as often as I used to. This is primarily a bed-and-breakfast place, and I used to stop here when I had business in the area." He paused. "Matter of fact, I was the one who suggested they start serving dinners, so you should thank me for the gourmet meal you're going to get."

"Oh? Am I getting a gourmet meal?" She hadn't seen a menu.

"Yes, and you needn't look for a menu. I've already ordered for you. Ah, here's the first course—a shrimp-and-celery salad. Your creation, Marty?" he asked as the waitress set their salads before them.

She smiled and nodded. "With my own special dressing. I hope you like it," she added anxiously.

"Wonderful!" Karin assured her when she'd sampled it. "A secret recipe?"

"Oh, no," Marty answered, naming the ingredients for the dressing, as well as for the clam chowder that was to follow. "I made the chowder, too," she said with pride.

"Nice kid," Karin said as the girl moved away. "And this is positively the most comfortable restaurant I've ever been in. It's like being in someone's home."

"In a way you are. It's a family business. Marty's the daughter." Blake went on to explain that the Reddicks had converted their big home into a bed-and-breakfast inn about three years ago when their son left for college. "Last year when Marty was ready for college, too, they said they needed more income, and I suggested this dinner arrangement, with reservations and orders placed in advance. That's the only way it could be handled on such a small scale, you see. Anyway, it's worked out pretty well."

"Yes, I can see it has," Karin said, thinking of the many times she'd heard variations on the theme of "Mr. Connors suggested..."

"Delicious," Blake said as he tasted the chowder. "Marty's pretty smart."

"You're pretty smart yourself, Mr. Connors. So the Reddicks are clients of yours?"

He looked surprised. "No, oh, no! No, they're just, well, not exactly friends, but I'd stayed with them a few times and we'd talk and—"

"Say no more." Karin held up a hand. "I see it all. Someone sings a sad song about a slump in his business and along comes the giveaway guy with the answer, be it just good advice or maybe a four-thousand-dollar check!" she said, twinkling at him.

"Come now. You make me sound like a sucker, a soft touch."

"No, no, but—" She broke off as Marty served the main course. Anyway, she didn't know quite what she'd intended to say.

He certainly wasn't the hard-nosed businessman she'd thought him. There was something about him... Yes, she had glimpsed it before, although it tended to get lost under that efficient, dollar-sign exterior. But it had become glaringly apparent to her this evening—that quality he had of genuine concern, generosity and goodwill toward others.

"I owe you an apology, Blake Connors," she said quite seriously. A lump rose in her throat, and trying to lighten the moment, she gave a gurgle of laughter. "I had you pegged right the first time—Santa Claus!"

He gave a sheepish grin. "Now you're pulling my leg. Just this afternoon you accused me of—"

"I was wrong." She suddenly found herself feeling genuinely happy and in a very festive mood. She pointed a finger at him. "Definitely Santa Claus. And with you, it's always Christmas!"

"And with you, Karin Palmer, everything's unpredictable. One minute you're a spitfire and the next..." He shrugged as if puzzled. "But never mind about that. This is the mood I like. When your eyes laugh and your dimples dance in that enchanting way." His smile made Karin blush and lower her eyes.

It was as if they'd absorbed the warm cheerful atmosphere of their surroundings, and for the moment all disagreement between them was forgotten. They talked and laughed easily, and Karin felt a strange contentment as the meal progressed. A delicious meal. She ate every morsel of the fresh sole that had been broiled in lemon sauce with capers.

"No dessert," she protested, but regained her appetite when a dish of juicy blackberry cobbler was set before her. "Perfect," she announced. "I'll bet Mrs. Reddick doesn't lack for return customers."

Blake said this was true, that they had many regular customers and often had to turn people away.

"You certainly gave the Reddicks the right advice. But that seems to be a habit with you." She leaned her chin on her hand and gave him a speculative look. "How does that make you feel?"

"What do you mean?"

"To always have the right answer—the sixth sense that enables you to guide Joe Blow or Mary Whatever straight up the ladder of success. Doesn't that make you feel like some kind of god?" She was half kidding and was surprised to see him start. "Hey, I didn't mean ... Did I say something I shouldn't?"

"No," he said, shaking his head. "It's just that, well, you're wrong. I don't always know what's right. And dealing with so many people can be scary when someone's success depends on you and you're not sure you're giving them the right direction."

"Oh?" She could tell he was troubled about something, but didn't want to pry. "Look," she said, "you're not really a god. I know that. You can only do or say what you feel is right."

He stared at her for a long time, then sighed. "Yeah. But I usually make quick judgments and I'm not always sure." He took a deep breath and leaned forward, as if making a decision to confide in her. "You see, I had a client who ran into some trouble with one of his customers. I looked into the matter and decided my client's actions were not quite kosher. Dumped him on the spot. Against the wishes of my staff, I might add. It's only one mistake, they argued. Give him a chance." He took another deep breath. "I didn't listen. I wanted no part of him."

"I think you were right," Karin said without hesitation. "Oh, I don't know the circumstances, but I know you and I've seen what goes on at New Ventures. I think the mark of your success is that every move you make is to improve or expand the services, but never at the expense of quality or human values." She folded her hands and regarded him earnestly. "Now, I may not know much about business, but I do know that some business people don't operate that way. Their emphasis is on increasing profits by undermining the competition or by cutting corners, which can be detrimental to the customer. I guess what I'm saying, Blake, is that, given the variety of people you deal with and the number of businesses at stake, you're better off without a client who doesn't have...integrity."

He looked into her eyes for a moment before murmuring a simple thank-you. However, he still seemed troubled, and when he spoke again, she guessed it was as much to himself as to her. "I suppose you're right. We weren't on the same wavelength and I couldn't work with him. But he's a young man on his way up, and I'd hate to have this one mistake ruin his future." Blake gave an uncomfortable shrug. "You see, it didn't quite end with my dropping him. Recently he had a bid in for a big job with an agency, and one of the guys on the board approached me. You know, 'Hey, Blake, what's the lowdown on so and so, wasn't he with you ... ?'"

Karin sat up. He must be talking about Jane's fiancé, the contractor. So Blake *was* approached! "What did you say?"

His expression was rueful. "Practically nothing. What could I say? 'Don't trust the creep'? Or, 'He's the greatest—give him the bid'? So I skirted the whole issue, and I've been wondering ever since...was I being unfair and, if so, to whom?"

Blake tapped his finger on the table and Karin thought she'd never seen him look so uncertain. His tense face did not reflect a self-serving businessman, but a human being agonizing over whether he'd done harm to another.

Impulsively she covered his hand with hers. "Listen to me, Blake Connors. You are not responsible for everyone in the entire world. Your client has to learn from his own mistakes, and your friend on the board is responsible for his own decisions." She smiled at him. "As I said, you're not really a god."

He turned his hand over to clasp hers. "And you're no angel, Karin Palmer. So why do you always make me feel so much ... at peace?"

"Oh, you!" she said, but for the second time that evening, a lump rose in her throat as he lifted her hand and pressed the palm to his lips. A warmth spread through her, and her fingers gently caressed his cheek before drawing away. But his eyes still held hers and she reveled in the wonderful silent communication contained in that clear steady gaze.

The spell was broken by Marty. "Your after-dinner drinks, Mr. Connors," she said as she served the liqueurs.

Blake lifted his glass. "To you, Karin Palmer. You're a very special person—and I plan to make you very rich."

She touched her glass to his, but smilingly shook her head. "I know you have the right answer for anyone who wants to get rich, but I keep telling you that's not my measure of success. So you needn't think you're going to con me into doing that relocation project."

"Did I say special? I guess I meant stubborn," he said, laughing, and she was glad to see that his mood had lightened. "Well, anyway, you're right about the variety of people and businesses I have to juggle, sometimes balancing one against the other. Here you are dragging your feet, and there's Snowden running so fast I'm afraid he's going to fall flat on his face."

"Oh?" She wrinkled her nose, which had been tickled by the brandy. "I didn't know Snowden was a client."

"He isn't now. But he was one of my first when I opened the Philadelphia branch. Guess I never let go."

"Right." She nodded, her eyes alight with mischief. "And 'incubator' is the proper name for your company. You're like a mother hen, worrying forever over your chicks, and it doesn't seem to matter whether you helped them out of the nest or kicked them out."

They carried on talking in this light and teasing manner, and later, Karin never knew what made her change her mind. Perhaps it was Blake's insistence that the relocation project would only be temporary. Perhaps it was his anxiety about Snowden; he seemed to feel that the man's whole operation was destined for failure if specially trained personnel could not be persuaded to relocate.

Whatever the reason, she found herself saying, "All right. I'll be here a few more days for workshops. But as soon as I return I'll give it a try."

"Great! I really appreciate this. And you won't try alone. I plan to work closely with you on this one."

It was then that her heart seemed to quicken and she felt a tingle of joyful anticipation.

CHAPTER TEN

HE HADN'T BEEN exactly truthful with her.

But, he argued with himself, he hadn't exactly lied, either. Snowden did need to relocate trained personnel. Still, Karin would never have taken on the project had he not represented Snowden as hovering on the brink of bankruptcy when, in fact, it was the other way around. K. Palmer Tours was the company badly in need of a financial boost. So, if she should benefit in the process . . . Oh, hell, he *had* done the right thing.

He decided that if the project was to be successful, he'd have to oversee it himself. He couldn't quite put his finger on it, but Vickie seemed to rub Karin the wrong way. Anyway, he had some ideas, a new approach to relocation tours, that he wanted to experiment with. This could be developed into a whole new industry, possibly worldwide.

They needed to get started right away, so the morning after Karin was due back from Mendocino he drove out to her house. He knew she was lukewarm on the project and thought it best to start their planning where they could be alone. Away from the office and Vickie.

As he rang the doorbell he thought that, even with this major project afoot, Karin would likely be busy at something else. If she wasn't out playing tennis he'd find her painting or maybe canning something or other.

"She's hunting for worms," said Meg, who opened the door. Looking cool, composed and quite beautiful despite her paint-spattered smock and the smudge of paint on her cheek, she spoke in her usual cheerful fashion. "How nice to see you, Mr. Connors. I'm taking a break and was just about to have a long cool drink. Come and join me."

He followed her into the family room and looked suspiciously at the pale green liquid she poured from a pitcher. Hunting for worms? "Is Karin planning to go fishing?" he asked as he took a cautious sip. Bland but not bad.

"Fishing?" Meg looked puzzled for a moment, then brightened. "Oh—worms! No, she's not going fishing. She's trying to save our tomatoes."

Now it was his turn to look puzzled.

"We found one of the plants completely devoured this morning," Meg explained. "Those tomato worms are voracious." She frowned. "I don't know why we call them worms. Actually they're caterpillars that'll soon be transformed into those big extraordinarily beautiful moths. Magnificent and colorful!" She shook her head. "You'd never believe they could develop from those creepy worms! So ugly! Big fat long green creatures, as green as this drink." She gestured toward his drink and seemed not to notice that Blake, who'd been about to take a swallow, lowered his glass. "That's why they're so hard to find, you see. Same color as the tomato plants, which they can consume in a flash." She sighed. "But when I think of those beautiful moths, I can't bear to destroy the worms. Bob's at a golf tournament, so it's up to Karin. Of course she won't destroy them, either. She'll leave that to the chickens."

"Chickens?" There was no end to the surprises in this household.

"Oh, yes. We have nine hens, excellent layers. So we always have fresh untainted eggs, you see. The worms are quite a treat for the hens. They'll gobble them up just like that." Meg snapped her fingers. "And we'll have our delicious sun-ripened untainted tomatoes. So, round and round it goes." She made a circular motion with her arm. "Isn't nature wonderful?"

"Yes, indeed." Blake set down his glass. He was not in the mood for another nature lecture. "I'll just go outside to find Karin. I have a few things to discuss with her." Like buses, brochures, and shopping districts for prospective Sacramentons!

"Of course. She's at the far end of the garden."

He hadn't realized how large the yard was. The swimming pool and well-tended lawn were separated by carefully spaced shrubs and flower beds from the oversize vegetable garden, where he finally came upon Karin, kneeling among the tomato plants. She looked like a grubby schoolboy in cutoff jeans and ragged T-shirt. Her back was to him, and she was searching diligently through the plants as if she had nothing on her mind but tomato worms. However, as he approached, she turned quickly.

"I think this is the last culprit," she said, holding out a stem on which was perched the fattest longest most disgusting worm he had ever seen. He winced.

"Oh, I thought you were Meg," Karin said, dropping the stem and worm into a can. "I didn't expect . . ." She looked a little flustered and didn't go on to voice the question in her eyes.

He answered it, anyway. "I came out so we could get started on the Snowden project. I expected you to call me when you got back to town."

"I was going to as soon as I got my business in order."

"Oh?" He looked significantly at the can of worms.

She flushed. "I meant my tour business! There's a watercolor session at Grass Valley that I had to make arrangements for and—"

"Snowden is tour business," he broke in. "And I'd say he ought to have priority."

"Really?" She lifted her chin defiantly. "Well, I'd say my already scheduled art tours should have priority. And I think you did mention in our original interview that New Ventures tenants were to retain their independence." She paused as if regretting her outburst. Awkwardly she rubbed an arm across her damp forehead and said, almost apologetically, "Anyway, I hadn't forgotten the Snowden business. I'd planned to start on it at the end of the week."

"The end of the week!" Did she have any idea how much work was involved? "Plans for this project should have been made weeks ago."

"I only agreed to take this on three days ago!"

"Okay. Okay. Right," he said, remembering that she thought she was doing Snowden—and him—a favor. "And I am grateful. I came out thinking I might help speed things on."

"Oh. Yes." She looked at the can on the ground beside her dirt-smudged thigh. "Well, let me just get rid of these."

He followed her to a small wire-fenced enclosure that he hadn't noticed before, so well was it concealed by vines. Someone had done some pretty clever landscaping, he thought. Not only was it esthetically pleasing, it provided for various unusual activities.

"Where do you keep the pigs?" he asked.

"Pigs?" Karin looked surprised, then laughed. "Oh, we have to draw the line somewhere. We're not really in the country." She emptied the contents of the can into the pen, and he stared in fascination as several clucking hens began to devour the worms.

Nature. Like Meg said, round and round it goes, he thought, trying to remember if he'd ever before in his life seen a real chicken.

Karin set the can down. "All right," she announced briskly. "We'll go back to the house and get started."

"Okay." But he stood quite still, absorbed in the scene before him. There was something about the quiet, the fresh country air, or perhaps the complacently strutting hens—something that engendered a strange sense of peace. He lingered a long moment before turning to follow her.

LATER, WHEN THEY WERE seated around a table on the patio, Karin frowned at Blake, feeling more than a little puzzled. "Capital? Why do you need to know that?" She had installed him in a cool spot, set out a pitcher of lemonade and joined him, regardless of the fact that she looked like a scarecrow. Why did he always seem to pop up when she was looking her worst? Anyway, she was quite prepared to discuss the tour schedules, yet the first thing he wanted to know was how much capital she had. If that meant cash . . . "I keep very little in reserve," she said. "Only about enough to lease the next bus."

"You'll need enough to lease several buses for this project," he said. "And you'll have to plunk down a hefty sum in advance to ensure delivery on such short notice. Oh, yes,'' he replied to the quizzical lift of her eyebrow, ''you'd be surprised at the arrangements money can make. And you'll need funds to pay your staff.''

''Staff?''

''Couldn't possibly handle it all by yourself. Three buses may roll at one time. There should be someone on each to relate essential information and distribute your brochures.''

''Brochures?''

''Yes. We'll have them printed up after we've assembled the information—real estate, shopping districts, schools, et cetera. Art galleries, too! And perhaps we'll need maps marking the best routes to—''

''Just a darn minute!'' Karin felt hot, grimy, overwhelmed and decidedly incensed. This was more than she'd bargained for. ''Look, I didn't realize this project was going to be so costly. I don't think—''

''Not costly. You can probably swing it for less than five thousand.''

''But I don't *have* five thousand!''

''Then we'll have to arrange financing.''

''I'm already financed up to the hilt. I haven't begun to pay back the two thousand I got from Uncle Bob.'' She decided not to mention the balance due on Mr. Turner's bus. But she certainly had no intention of adding to her debts.

He leaned back in his chair and shook his head. ''Why are you thinking of cost instead of proceeds? Do you realize you'd gross more than twenty thousand on this one venture? And there are other companies planning to—''

''Twenty thousand dollars?'' She couldn't believe it. ''I thought you said this Mr. Snowden was in difficulty. How can he afford to make that kind of outlay?''

"He can't afford not to make it. It's very pertinent to his expansion and is a very small percentage of the total cost of the operation." Blake gave a little cough. "And I didn't mean to imply that he was in financial difficulty. Just that this expansion is risky. There's a lot at stake..." He spread his hands. "It takes money to make money. And, unlike Snowden, your profit is guaranteed. You'll get paid at the onset of the tours."

"*If* I had the five thousand to invest, which I don't." She wasn't sure she wanted to get into this venture, after all.

"Don't worry about that. I'll take care of the financing."

"Oh. All right." She relaxed a bit, thinking. She hated to assume more debt, but she could repay it as soon as—

"Of course, I'll require some security."

"Of course." Proper business procedures were essential with New Ventures. She liked that. "An increase in the percentage of profits or interest on the loan?"

"Neither. I was thinking more in terms of something of value to hold now—just in case the deal falls through."

"Falls through!" She sat up. "But you said it was a sure thing, that the income was guaranteed!"

He was in the midst of swallowing and half choked. He cleared his throat, then set down his glass. "Well, yes, it is. But in business..." Again he spread his hands. "We have to be prepared for all contingencies."

"Then the deal is off. I don't have anything of value."

"Oh, but you have. You have something I want very much. Something only you can give me." Now he was smiling. No. He was leering at her!

Flushing, she instinctively pushed back her chair. Well, hadn't she known all along! A man who'd send a big check to a woman he'd met in a bar...

"Some things are not for sale, Mr. Connors."

"Everything has a price, Ms. Palmer, and I'm willing to pay whatever yours is. I *am* rich, you know." His very words on that first day! She drew herself up, burning, ready to lash out at him, hardly hearing his next words. "You must have other paintings. Surely you could part with the one of the Devil's Punch Bowl."

She shut her mouth, speechless, overcome by a tumult of emotions—chagrin, relief, amusement. And then annoyance. He'd been putting her on.

He grinned. "Had you going, didn't I?"

"Not really," she said, casually examining her nails. "Just amazed. Anyone who'd pay more than five dollars for any painting of mine is a nut, not a connoisseur."

Now he laughed heartily. "Okay. So I'm a nut."

"True," she agreed, trying to join in the laughter, trying to hide her pleasure. He wanted one of her paintings!

That afternoon was a prelude to many similar planning sessions. Together they consulted city maps and real-estate pamphlets. They visited shopping districts, schools, parks and recreational facilities. Together they devised their own maps and information brochures, mapped out the tour routes, interviewed and hired two young college women who would serve as part-time guides. Karin wasn't really surprised that Blake spent an inordinate amount of time with the owner of one small independent tour company; she knew it was his policy to help any of his clients who had special problems. The setup for relocation tours was different from her art tours, and she felt grateful for his expertise. She was glad when she could reward him with a dinner that included Meg's garden-fresh vegetables, or perhaps coax him to relax with a swim in the pool after a particularly busy day.

Not that it was all fun and games. They had a few heated discussions.

The first came as they sat at the big dining table, which was loaded with maps and sample brochures.

"This won't do," Blake told her. "You'd better move into the complex. There's a vacant space now in Complex One that'll just about accommodate your needs."

"I don't want to move into the complex. I like working here."

"I know you do." He shook his head in exasperation. "So anytime you feel like it you can run out to pick tomatoes—or maybe worms to feed the chickens—or God knows what else!"

"So what's wrong with that?" she challenged. "It's like taking a breather, relaxing for a minute and—"

"It just happens to be a crazy way to run a business, which, incidentally, is what you're trying to do. And look at this," he added, gesturing at the pile of papers. "I'm sure this table is used to accommodate all kinds of junk . . . paraphernalia," he hastily amended. "But you need to be more organized. You need to file your brochures and information pamphlets."

"I've got a file cabinet in my room."

"Probably already loaded with material about museums, art exhibits and the like!"

This was true, so she said nothing.

"Besides," he went on, "you're hiring additional staff to help conduct these tours, and while you're familiar with the tour route, they're not. You'll have to schedule training sessions, and where will you hold those? I hope you don't expect your employees to drive way out here. Not to mention that it might interfere with whatever activities your aunt and uncle are engaged in. That wouldn't be fair to Meg and Bob, would it?"

His arguments sounded so logical that she finally gave in. "But," she said, frowning, "it seems like an awful lot of trouble for just a temporary project."

"Well, now," he said, pushing back his chair, "it may not be temporary. I've been thinking. There's a real market for this kind of service. And not only for the purpose of relocating personnel. Company executives are always scouting around for the best area in which to locate and—"

"Just a moment!" She sat up straight. "We had an understanding that this was only a temporary activity for my company. Besides, I'm no expert in this field."

"You could be. And the potentials for this kind of service are—"

"I don't care what the potentials are."

He threw down his pen. "Karin, what the hell have you got against success?"

"People have different notions of success, Blake Connors. You only rate a business successful if it's growing and expanding. Some people are content to operate on an even keel."

"You're the only one I know who prefers stagnation to growth!"

She flinched. "That's not the right term. And I'm not the only one. Many people would rather operate on a small scale."

"Name one."

"Well, there's Dolly, for example."

"Dolly Spencer? You're wrong there, my girl. Right now she's all excited about placing her goods in a chain of grocery stores."

"*You're* excited. She's going along with you, but she's not all that happy about it."

"What gave you that idea?" He stared at her, a very grave look on his face. Karin flushed. She had spoken on impulse and now felt guilty. She had no right to discuss Dolly's business. But at his next words, "Well, come on, tell me why you think that," she felt compelled to explain.

"It's not what I think. It's what she said." Blake was so obviously crestfallen that she reached out a hand to touch his arm. "It's nothing against you or your ideas. She's extremely grateful for the way you've helped her. She says that for the first time in her life she doesn't have to worry about living expenses or the tuition for Keith's college. But she says she's satisfied with that."

"Satisfied? Look, she could have a million-dollar business. One her son could inherit."

"But don't you see, Blake? That's not what she wants. And it's certainly not what Keith wants. His interests lie in an entirely different direction. But more important is what's happening right now." Karin hesitated a moment, needing to put it just right. "It's not easy to be a single mother, Blake. You need time. Time to go to your kid's basketball game or see that he gets his homework done, or maybe just take a breather. Oh, I guess what I'm trying to say is that living is just as important as *earning* a living, and you have to balance one against the other. Making a million dollars doesn't always take priority."

Blake still had that grave look on his face, and then he shrugged. "Okay. Point taken." Then he grinned at her. "So what's *your* excuse? You're not a single mother. Anyway, we're not trying to make a million dollars. Right now we're just trying to put your business in the black. So let's get on with it. What do you think of this brochure?"

CHAPTER ELEVEN

"I'M CERTAINLY GLAD the Snowden relocation tours are finally launched." Vickie's dulcet tones failed to mask her vexation when, two weeks later, she faced Blake across the conference-room table. "Now perhaps we can proceed with the real business of New Ventures."

"Oh, I'd supposed the real business proceeded as usual during my absence under the capable management of my two faithful assistants." Blake smiled at her, well aware that he had missed the last two Thursday night "board" sessions he, Vickie and Pete usually held. "It's so reassuring to know I can always count on you to carry on."

"We can do with fewer of your compliments and more of your company," she answered. "Honestly, Blake, you know there are some things only you can handle, like the financing for Blascoe Tool and—"

"Oh, lay off, Vickie!" Pete broke in. "I checked with Wells Fargo, and the Blascoe deal is in the bag. And Blake is entitled to a breather."

Blake smiled. That was exactly what Karin called those untimely but undeniably pleasant little intervals when they saw to the chickens or took a dip in the pool or—

"A breather! Is that what you call it?" Vickie's nose twitched. "I'd call it working beyond the call of duty, trying to shore up the routine business of one of our most unproductive tenants. We're management consultants, not employees."

"Turkey—that's yours, Vickie. Pastrami, Pete. And mine is the ham on rye." Blake distributed the sandwiches that had been delivered from a nearby deli.

"Really, Blake, I do think you're setting a bad precedent," Vickie said as she unwrapped her sandwich. "Other tenants will begin to expect that same kind of attention."

"Hmm." Blake opened a can of cola and looked down at the agenda she'd prepared. Vickie was damned efficient. Competent, dependable and decorative. Decorative enough to attract some man who—he hoped—would mellow her. If that man could get past the cattiness... Blake grinned. Considering her capabilities, he chose to ignore that catty streak of hers. Anyway, she was right, he conceded as he took a swallow from the can. He *had* been spending too much time with Karin, and to tell the truth, it had been more of a breather than business. Of course she'd needed initial guidance, but once he got her on track, he just couldn't let go. Perhaps because of her crazy household, so different from anything he'd ever experienced in his apartment living. Everybody always busy at something, but looking as if they were just playing. Enjoying themselves. Maybe, Blake thought, that had drawn him in. He had found himself pulling weeds or practicing with Bob on his homemade golf tee, discussing some bizarre idea with Meg, critiquing her paintings or partaking of her health food and drinks.

But the best times had been with Karin. Of course there had been some lazy times, sitting around or swimming in the pool, but they'd taken care of business, too, drafting brochures, mapping out routes, exploring places he'd never considered.

"Pizza parlors and bowling alleys?" he had queried. "Why should we look at those?"

"People will want to know where their teenagers are going to hang out," she'd answered. He could see her now, laughing up at him, tomato juice dripping from her chin.

"So, what's wrong with that?" Pete's voice, louder than usual, broke into his reverie. He awoke to a heated discussion between Vickie and Pete. They were debating which of the four new applicants should occupy the three spaces that were soon to be vacated.

"I think we should put Lowell's Printing on hold," Vickie said now. "We don't have the room, and I'm doubtful about taking it on, anyway. There's a print shop on almost every corner in this town."

"So it comes down to who's tops," Pete argued. "Lowell does quality work, and I think we should promote him."

"Instead of the image consultant? The very first thing you have to present in business is yourself and—"

"No way," said Pete. "You present a product!"

"Right," Vickie responded sweetly. "Something new and different. This is an entirely new kind of service. Not old hat like—"

"Wait a minute, you two!" Blake interrupted. "Perhaps we can take them both on. I think we'll have another graduate soon. Dolly's Desserts."

"What?" Vickie exclaimed as both turned to Blake in surprise.

"But we've just decided to expand into grocery stores!" Pete said.

"Seems she's not interested in expanding, and I don't want to push her."

Both Vickie and Pete argued that Mrs. Spencer had certainly not reached her maximum. "The commercial potentials are endless," Pete said.

But Blake was firm. "She's been a good client, made the progress she desires, and we'll let her go with grace and goodwill," he said, his tone decisive.

As the session was about to break up, Blake turned to Pete. "You say this Lowell does quality printing?"

"The best."

"I'd like to check him out." Blake spread several pieces of paper, about the size of three-by-five index cards, on the table. "What do you think of these?"

Vickie came around to stand beside him, and she and Pete examined the papers. At the top of each was a cartoon of a dog engaged in some capricious activity, along with a telling caption.

"Oh, these are darling!" Vickie exclaimed. "I like this one where he's just kicked over the wastebasket." She read the caption aloud. " 'I'm sorry I upset you.' And look at the dog's expression! He really looks sorry."

"I could use this one right now," Pete said, pointing. An apologetic dog was gazing up from a broken vase, and the caption read, "Can't we patch things up?" "Thelma's giving me the silent treatment just because I said the living room didn't need redoing. Women!"

"Lovers!" Vickie said. "Can't you see these as a packet of correspondence for lovers? Look at this one where he's cuddled with the cat."

"That's rather what I had in mind," said Blake. "Pete, you get Lowell to do the packet for me. And Vickie, get hold of publicity—have them do a magazine ad for mail orders."

"And file it under what? I presume this is a new client?"

"Possibly," answered Blake. He'd have to check the legalities of doing business with a minor. "For now, take all expenses from my personal account. And file it un-

der 'Cookie Capers.''' Kind of cutesy. But that had been
Keith's choice and who was he to argue with such a talented kid?

THE RELOCATION TOURS were a tremendous success. Mr.
Snowden sent Karin flowers, a bonus and a thank-you
note for solving his personnel problems.

And Blake took her out to celebrate. He chose a restaurant with a lively rock-and-roll band, and she suspected he must have bribed the leader, for after every
three numbers they belted out an exhilarating version of
"Celebrate." Karin and Blake danced and danced and
danced. Like a couple of teenagers. And in between
dances he told her how wonderful she was.

"You have an infectious enthusiasm and an open
honest face. That's a powerful combination. Snowden
tells me he has people begging to be relocated in Sacramento." He raised his glass. "Here's to you, Karin."

"And to you." Karin lifted her own glass to touch his.
"You know I couldn't have done it without your help.
Thank you."

"Don't thank me. I told you that's my job. But working with someone who's got your talents and ingenuity
sure makes it easy. I'm going to have fun making you
rich, Karin Palmer. No, don't say it." He held up his
hand to ward off her protests. "Just tell me one thing.
What do you have against making a lot of money?"

"I suppose..." She hesitated, taken aback by his serious expression. "I guess I never thought about it. Guess
I never got beyond just making a living."

He put down his glass and shook his head. "Karin,
Karin," he said softly. "Do you know that's the trouble
with most people? They don't think big. Of course, there
are those who'd never get beyond the ordinary. But

you're different." He leaned forward and spoke with intensity. "You have all the attributes for spectacular success. Not only intelligence and ingenuity but an innate graciousness." He continued in this vein, and she drank in every word, reveling in the praise, exulting in the admiration radiating from his eyes. She felt confident, even inspired.

Later, when they were alone, sitting on the couch in her quiet living room, he said again, "I'm so proud of you, Karin."

She smiled at him, but her thank-you caught in her throat. In the mellow glow from the table lamp, every strong feature of his face was clearly visible, and she thought she read a question in the quirk of his brow, a message in his vivid blue eyes. When he took her in his arms, tenderly brushing her lips with his, her whole body responded, and she reached up to touch his face with a trembling hand, to trace a caressing finger along his jaw. His quickly drawn breath, his whispered "Karin, oh, Karin!" sent a sensation of pure pleasure through her. The sweet intoxicating sensuality enveloping her was heightened by the knowledge that she could please him. Her fingers tangled in his hair as she cradled his neck and pulled him closer. He deepened the kiss with a seductive fervor, and when his mouth traveled to the hollow of her throat she wanted to melt into him, to yield in total abandonment.

After a long moment he drew away, and she could tell he was trying to control his emotions.

"You're very special to me, Karin," he said as he tucked a curl behind her ear. She was grateful for the protective gesture. It was as if he was trying to lighten the atmosphere between them and give her time to sort out her own feelings.

"You're pretty special to me, Mr. C." Her voice was teasingly casual, but her heart was full, and she grappled with a sudden realization. She loved Blake Connors. She fell silent, absorbed in the joy and wonder of this truth, which until now she hadn't dared face.

Blake, too, was silent, seemingly absorbed in his own thoughts. He got up and moved toward the darkened window. She couldn't see his face, but she could tell his shoulders had tensed. Was she imagining it or was he struggling with some inner turmoil? Impulsively she went over and touched his arm. He turned quickly, taking both her hands in his.

"We're going to make K. Palmer Tours a stupendously successful company," he said, his voice brisk and positive in the old manner, his eyes bright with a promise—and a message? She smiled, concentrating on the "we." They would do it together. "I have grand plans," he said, with a reassuring wink.

She nodded. He was so imaginative, so innovative and efficient. She loved working with him. More than that, she loved *him* and would do all she could to make his grand plans succeed.

It was in this state of euphoria that, during the following months of September and October, Karin adhered to Blake's every suggestion. And she was rewarded. It was as if one success engendered yet another. No sooner had she finished with the Snowden tours than she was asked to do relocation tours for another company that was moving into the area. It was in a different part of town, necessitating new maps and tour routes, but the basic itinerary was the same and she knew how to handle it. She received contracts for relocation tours in nearby cities and tours for conventions in Sacramento. She even conducted a two-day private tour for a man from Scotland who was being courted by one of the big Sacramento companies. He was a golfer and she arranged for him to inspect golf courses within a hundred-mile radius.

By the time the cool crisp days of autumn with its intermittent rains had begun, Karin was spending most of her time in her office at the New Ventures complex. Business had escalated to such an extent that she was inundated with paperwork. She could never have managed without the big desk and several filing cabinets, not to mention the telephone and billing services and, of course, her staff, which now consisted of half a dozen college students who fit the tour jobs in between classes and assignments. If she wasn't at the office making preparations for one tour, she was out scouting areas for another.

She had assumed that being in the complex meant she would see more of Blake. Actually she saw less. He was often out of town, and when he was at New Ventures, he was usually closeted in his big office. Occasionally she'd catch a glimpse of him walking with Pete or Vickie as they left the office, presumably for lunch or some meeting. Karin tried to stifle the quick stab of jealousy, tried not to be haunted by a recurring vision of beautiful exotic Vickie leaning seductively toward Blake, touching him. Of course they'd have consultations and attend meetings together! She was his personal assistant, Karin reminded herself, bending to stuff a folder into the bottom drawer of a filing cabinet. She stood and kicked the drawer shut, trying to block out a nagging question. *How personal?*

At times, when she traced a finger along a map route or drove through an area to check out a pizza parlor or a shopping district, she couldn't help reliving the days she and Blake had done this together. And she missed him achingly. It was ridiculous to feel so bereft, she told herself. He had taken the time to train her and now she could do it alone. And if she saw him less frequently it was because he was as busy as she. Besides, he did seek her out when he could manage the time. He had stopped by the house three times, had twice taken her to lunch, and one memorable night to dinner. When she did see him, the magic was still here. He told her he was very proud of her, that she had created a new specialty and K. Palmer Tours was about to become a national byword. He said she'd soon be scheduling relocation tours in cities throughout the country. It was true she was becoming phenomenally successful. Her reputation was well established and she was making more money than she'd ever thought possible.

She should be ecstatic, Karin told herself one bleak October day. She stood at her office window staring out at the gathering mist. But she couldn't lift herself out of a deep feeling of depression. Silly! Just because she wasn't on the tour bus now making its way toward the deYoung Museum to view the display of holiday art. She felt hemmed in by the load of paperwork she had to get through and the preparations she had to make for the training session she was to hold in the morning—things only she could do. She'd much rather be on that bus.

Oh, darn it, she was getting to be a regular crybaby. But she loved the holidays, all of them. Even Halloween. She knew the tour group would stop at the Nut Tree for breakfast and to view the pumpkin-patch exhibit of witches, ghosts and black cats. Last year she'd made sketches of the haunted house.

Then they'd go on to the museum, to enjoy its always wonderful display of creative ideas. And with Thanksgiving and Christmas almost here . . .

Christmas. Her absolute favorite time of year. When she was a child... Of course, it was every child's favorite time. She remembered the anticipation, the excitement, the offerings she'd left for Santa Claus. But even as an adult she loved the season. The joy and warm hospitality of the day itself, spent with those you loved, was never an anticlimax for Karin, although she loved the busy days of preparation. Last year she and Meg had done their own Christmas cards, tiny original oil paintings on each. And they'd made Mr. and Mrs. Santa Claus rag dolls. Oh, for goodness' sake, what did she need with new ideas? She'd be lucky if she had time to do any decorating at all this year!

"Hey, Karin! Got something for you!" The door burst open, and Karin looked up to see Keith, a wide grin on his face.

"Keith, what are you doing out of school?"

"Had a dental appointment. Mom's taking me back to school, but she said I could stop in to bring you this and tell you the news."

"News? And a present?" she said, smiling as she took the wrapped package.

"It's not much. Just something because...aw, man...well, like, you started the whole thing."

"Oh?"

"Yeah. You said I could make money with my pencil. Remember?"

She nodded and he told her how Mr. Connors had taken the cartoons of Cookie and helped set up the captions. "And, man, I didn't even know he had them printed and packaged and took out an ad in some magazine and, man, orders are coming in like everything and I'm making money just like you said I could!"

She stared at him, trying to take it all in. He pointed a finger. "Open it. It's just . . . well, funny."

"Oh, Keith, that's wonderful! I'm so proud of you," she said as she slipped off the ribbon and unwrapped his offering. "But you didn't have to give me any—" She broke off and burst out laughing as she gazed at the colorful caricature of herself gawking up at Blake Connors, her big eyes exaggerated and a moony expression on her face. "Oh, Keith," she muttered, trying to catch her breath. "I don't know whether to thank you or murder you!"

"I wanted to buy you a present, but . . . well, my money's all tied up. Man, I was all set to buy Mom and you something and get me a pair of Nikes. But Mr. Connors said hold it. He set me up a bank account under a company name—Cookie Capers—but he says it takes money to make money. And we're going to capitalize on the current craze and have these cups and T-shirts made— you know, like with the caricatures and captions. Man!" For a moment Keith looked quite overwhelmed by the thought of this enterprise. "Anyway," he said at last, "Mom said you'd like it . . . even if . . . Well, it's funny." He looked a little anxious. "I did it that time we were in Mendocino."

"I love it!" she said, giving him a reassuring smile.

He looked relieved. "Well . . . good. Hey, I did one for Mr. Connors, too!"

"Oh? Just like this?" she asked hesitantly. Oh, Lord! Please, no. Not with her looking like some lovesick groupie gazing at her adored rock star!

"Aw, man, no. But his is funny, too. I've got him standing by his desk pointing his finger like . . . you know, like he's always telling somebody what to do and there's

all this money coming from everywhere—bills on his desk
and pouring out of his pockets..."

"Oh, Keith, that's perfect," she said with a relieved
chuckle.

"Yeah. Well, I'd better split. See you," Keith said, and
disappeared.

Karin stared thoughtfully after him. No doubt about
it. He was one perceptive kid. And he had an amazing
ability to portray that perception on paper. She looked
down at the carefully framed picture, her pride in Keith
battling with her own chagrin at having her feelings so
clearly perceived and displayed. With acute embarrassment, she hid the portrait in the bottom drawer of her
desk and returned to her task.

It was slow going. Every few minutes she would find
herself holding a packet of brochures and staring into
space. Keith was right about Blake, too. He did have a
knack for making money—and helping others to make
money. Who else would have conceived the idea of turning Keith's drawings of his dog into such a lucrative project? Who else would have so generously guided him? But
that was Blake. She thought of the friend whose beauty-
supply business had been rescued from the trunk of his
car. She thought of the man with the bad back whose
floundering seed company had been directed into a million-dollar mail-order business. She thought of herself.
And with a blinding flash of insight, she realized she was
just another project. Blake wasn't interested in Karin
Palmer, but in K. Palmer Tours.

CHAPTER TWELVE

"I'M GOING TO MISS YOU," Karin said when she came in one day about three weeks later and found Dolly packing.

"Oh, don't worry," Dolly responded cheerfully. "I'll still supply your muffins. I'm opening up this little shop on J Street, and Sally's still going to work with me." She handed Karin a card with her new address. "I'm not quitting, I'm graduating from New Ventures."

"But I don't see why you're pulling out now," said Jane, who walked in at that moment. "Seems to me your business was just starting to grow."

Dolly laughed. "This—New Ventures—is only a launching pad. And the way I see it, I'm launched. The dessert concessions for the hotels provide a regular basic income, and I can take on whatever small catering jobs I choose. That's enough for me. I want to have time to play a little bridge, stay home with Keith or go to some of his games. Pass me that stack of muffin tins, Karin."

Karin did so, her thoughts on Dolly's words. *Time.* To do what you wanted to do. "I know what you mean," she said slowly.

"Well, I don't!" Jane snapped. "Connors has some great plans for me and I plan to stick with him."

Karin gave her a quick glance. So, Blake Connors was back in her good graces.

Jane caught her glance and grinned. "Yeah, I finally saw the light." She held up her left hand. The flashy diamond was missing.

"Oh, I'm sorry," Karin said automatically.

"Don't be. I'm well out of that one. Believe me, whatever Connors did to Jack, the sneak deserved it!"

"Oh, Blake didn't...wouldn't..." Karin broke off just in time. "Here, I'll help you close that," she told Dolly. To her relief, the conversation seemed to be forgotten as the three of them struggled to tape down the flaps of the large carton. She certainly had no business discussing the issue, but she was glad Jane was no longer taken in by the unknown Jack Austin. No, it wasn't just that. She was also glad that Jane finally understood—and admitted— that Blake Connors was a fair man.

He is fair, she thought disconsolately. All he'd ever said was that she was "special," and that they were going to make K. Palmer Tours a "special" company. It wasn't his fault that she'd presumed more.

"I did consider expanding, the way Mr. Connors suggested," Dolly confided when Jane had left. "Build it into a business for Keith, you know. But I never thought he was all that interested in baking. Anyway, he has his own enterprise now. And he's just turned sixteen! Can you believe it?"

"I think it's wonderful," Karin replied.

"You deserve the credit, Karin," Dolly said, straightening up from the packing case. "You started it all."

"Nonsense," Karin said, a little embarrassed. "All I did—"

"Was take his hobby seriously, which neither I nor Keith ever did. So it's all your fault that my dining table has become a drawing board and his artwork's scattered all over the house!" Dolly shook her finger, pretending to scold.

"Oh, you poor, poor baby!" Karin smiled, seeing the pride in Dolly's face.

Dolly returned her smile. "So get us some coffee, will you, Karin? I need a rest. And I want to ask you something." She sank into one of the chairs.

Karin filled two cups and went to sit beside Dolly.

"You know that studio your aunt has in her attic?" Dolly asked. When Karin nodded, she said, "I'm going to have our attic made into a studio for Keith, and I want you to help me plan it. You know what's needed."

"Great!" Karin entered enthusiastically into the plan, hardly aware of her deepening envy. Time and space to do the things you enjoy...

IT WASN'T THE FIRST art seminar she'd had to miss. The art tours were becoming fewer, crowded out by the more lucrative relocation and convention tours. And because of her other duties, Karin had been compelled to leave most of the actual guiding to her assistants, the college students who worked for her on a freelance basis.

But she'd planned to go to Malibu, hoping it would lift her out of the persistent depression that had been plaguing her. Three days away from the dreary Northern California rain. Three days under the tutelage of Madeline Kolensky, the renowned watercolorist. Karin could learn so much from her. And three days to enjoy the sun, the sea and the sand.

But organizing the relocation tours scheduled for the electronics plant being opened in Stockton couldn't be delayed. It was, unfortunately, the kind of planning she could entrust only to herself. And in Stockton. She didn't even like Stockton!

That morning, just before her departure for Stockton, she sat at breakfast with her aunt and uncle, feeling unhappy, frustrated and ashamed.

"I'm just being lazy," she muttered.

"That's all right. Everybody's entitled to one vice," Meg said complacently. "Mine is drinking coffee," she added as she poured another cup of the steaming brew. "I know it's not good for me, but I enjoy it too much to give it up."

"Well, I don't enjoy being lazy. Or at least I *can't* enjoy it," Karin said as she stabbed a segment of grapefruit. "I have to go to Stockton and prowl through shopping malls and subdivisions when I'd rather be lying on the beach at Malibu, maybe doing a little painting. I'd even rather hang around here and help you clear out the flower beds."

Meg laughed. "Aha! You're not lazy. You're like me—you love to putter. You're interested in so many things you can't concentrate too long on just one. And there's nothing wrong with that!"

"Except of course when it comes to making a living."

"So we're back to that." Meg looked intently at her niece before she said, "You can be a slave to a business, as well as to a paycheck, you know."

At this, Bob laid down his newspaper. "Don't listen to Meg. Unless you happen to be independently wealthy, you free-spirited putterers need someone to support your puttering. Some sucker like me who *is* a slave to a paycheck."

"Men!" Meg exclaimed. "It takes more than money to make a living, Bob Palmer, and don't you forget it." She wagged a finger at him. "My puttering has kept you healthy and happy and very well fed!"

"Okay, okay, so there's a balance." Bob got up to kiss his wife. "But you must admit money's essential, sweetheart. Maybe Karin had better marry that tennis player who's been after her and let him support her." He laughed as he picked up his newspaper and left the room.

"I don't think that's quite what Richard has in mind." Karin grinned at Meg. "His idea is that we should shack up and share alike."

"Oh, I see." Meg lifted an eyebrow. "In the modern way. Well, I suppose there's nothing wrong with that. If it's your choice. Is it?"

"I'm afraid it's too late for me to make a choice."

"Oh?"

"Richard's moved in with Joyce. She and Al broke up, and Richard seems to feel the urge to comfort her."

"I see." Meg looked keenly at Karin. "Does that bother you?"

"Good heavens, no! In fact I'm rather relieved." Karin pushed back her coffee cup and sighed. "I like Richard, but only as a friend. I knew he wanted more, and I suppose it was unfair of me to spend so much time with him." She hesitated. "The thing is, he's lots of fun and took my mind off... off other things."

Meg continued to study her. "So if it's not Richard, who is it?"

"Nobody," she said, quickly erasing the image of Blake Connors from her mind. "I mean, whatever gave you that idea?"

"You've been so down in the dumps lately. And that's not like you."

"Oh, Meg, I don't think I'm cut out to run a business, after all. I'm sick of prowling through residential areas and shopping centers and putting my observations on paper, then telling my guides where to go and what to say about what I put on paper. Boring!'' She stood up and threw down her napkin, then was instantly contrite. ''I'm sorry. I shouldn't complain. Things are going so well. Darn it! I guess I am lazy.''

''Or too involved,'' Meg said quietly.

Karin, who had started away, turned back. ''What do you mean 'too involved,' Aunt Meg?''

''Well, you know, two men, two businesses, and not enough time to sort them out.''

''Oh, no, Meg, you're wrong. It's not—'' She stopped, unable to refute the truth. Dear sweet zany Meg was as perceptive as Keith. ''Guess I've got some thinking to do, huh?''

''I'd say so.'' Meg was pouring another cup of coffee and didn't look up.

''Thanks.'' Karin bent to kiss her aunt's cheek before going out.

She drove along Highway Five, deep in thought. Meg was right. Two men. Richard and Blake. Richard, naturally, was out of the picture now, if indeed he'd ever really been in it.

Be honest, Karin. Of course he was in the picture. He'd been a welcome diversion. A good tennis partner or theater companion, who teased, flattered and, yes, for a few hours at a time, helped divert her mind from Blake.

Blake. Dear Lord, how had she allowed herself to become so involved? She had never meant to. That very first day when she'd come under his spell at lunch, she had sensed the danger of his magnetism and had vowed to avoid him.

If he hadn't come out to the house, hadn't persuaded her to join New Ventures... She felt a flash of pure rage. He had followed her all the way to Mendocino. He had charmed, cajoled and misdirected her into these boring relocation tours!

Her fingers tightened on the wheel. Blake. Would she be bored if *he* was beside her? No, she wouldn't; the answer required no deliberation. Just being with him made her feel exhilarated and keenly alive. There was an aura of joy about any activity shared with him. And when he kissed her... A surge of passion flooded through her, and she felt an almost painful longing. And always, there was that tug at her heart, that wish to please him. She knew she would willingly do almost anything he asked.

But he asked nothing. Even though she could tell he was as moved as she was by their brief intimacies, she sensed a certain reticence. And all he'd ever said was that she was "special." And yes, something else. "I'm going to have fun making you rich, Karin Palmer."

His dream. Not hers.

Two businesses. One that bored, entrapped—and made her rich. One that afforded travel, art, leisure—and made her happy.

A simple choice. She'd rather be happy than rich.

Still, a persistent question nagged at her.

Suppose Blake had said "Let's get married," or "Come and live with me"? Or even if he mentioned that magic word—love. Again the nameless longing assailed her. Still, she knew it wouldn't be enough. She would only be half a person if she wasn't free to follow her own dream, pursue her own interests. She wouldn't be happy. Nor could she make anyone else happy.

So, that morning as she pulled into the central area of Stockton, she made up her mind. This would be her last relocation tour.

CHAPTER THIRTEEN

BLAKE WAS LOOKING at her as if he couldn't believe his ears. "What do you mean, you're leaving New Ventures?" he sputtered.

Karin swallowed. She hadn't intended to break away from New Ventures, at least not yet. She liked the setup, liked having her reservations and bookkeeping handled through them. She'd said this to Vickie before Blake came into the conference room.

Vickie had stared at her in open amazement. "My dear Karin, we aren't a maintenance crew, you know. Our aim is advancement, improvement, *progress.*"

Karin had awkwardly fingered the prospectus she'd been discussing with Vickie. She wished Pete was there. Vickie always made her feel like an idiot at these management meetings.

"But I intend to make progress," she'd said. "In my original direction. Art."

Vickie had flashed her superior smile. "That doesn't make any sense at all. Mr. Connors and I decided long ago that those art tours are losers."

Karin, vividly reminded of Blake's reference to "artsy losers" that day in Mendocino, had momentarily lost track of Vickie's next words. But the memory nettled, and she'd strengthened her resolve. So when Vickie had congratulated her on the successful completion of the Stockton project and said, "Surely you realize that these relocation tours are your money-makers. Of course you'll accept this bid from the Simco Corporation.''

Karin's answer had been a firm "No!"

It was then that Vickie had started her spiel about progress versus maintenance. "It appears that we, at New Ventures, are wasting our time. And really, if you're not interested in expanding your business and thereby increasing our profits, then it's in your own best interest to withdraw from us.''

Karin listened, struggling with her emotions. Withdraw from New Ventures? From Blake?

"But I am interested in expanding,'' she said defensively, reluctant to break this tenuous tie to Blake. Blake *was* New Ventures, and she enjoyed working with him. He made her feel competent, capable—special. "As I told you," she said, tapping the folder, "I'll be concentrating more on art seminars and—''

"Art seminars!'' Vickie spit out as if it had a bad taste. "Really, Karin, we'd be working at cross-purposes!''

"But if I could make them pay…'' Karin's voice trailed off, alerted by her conscience. Her own purpose was pretty crossed up. It wasn't to work with Blake but to be with him. Because he made her feel alive and happy.

"Don't you see? We're pulling in different directions and that's unproductive,'' Vickie said.

And unfair, thought Karin. Unfair to Blake, whose whole aim was progress. *Unfair to me, too,* she thought, *when what I want is something entirely different.*

"Yes. Perhaps it *would* be best for me to withdraw,'' Karin had said thoughtfully, feeling confused. That was when Blake entered the conference room. He had evidently come in search of Vickie, whose presence he seemed to forget when he encountered Karin.

"Karin!" he'd said. "I didn't know you were here. Do you have time for lunch?"

"I . . . I don't know," she answered, still reeling from the turn of events. And the sight of Blake. Brimming with vitality and good spirits, the laughter lines crinkling around his eyes. "Well, yes, I—"

Vickie stood abruptly, pushing back her chair. "Best to tell him now, dear," she said, nodding at Karin.

"Tell me what?" Blake looked from one to the other.

"She's leaving us," Vickie announced brusquely.

"Leaving?" Blake asked, and Karin squirmed under the puzzled accusation in his eyes. "Why? What's the problem?"

"It's her own decision, Blake. A prerogative of all our tenants. And of course we'll release her—with grace and goodwill." Vickie walked over to place a soothing hand on Blake's arm before turning to Karin. "I'll get the paperwork started, dear, and the best of luck to you." She swept from the room, a smile of smug satisfaction on her face.

Blake had not taken his eyes from Karin. "I repeat," he said now. "Why this talk about leaving us? What brought this on?"

"It's just that Vickie thought . . . I mean, we decided, well, since I'm not going to do any more relocation tours—"

"Sure you are." He relaxed visibly. "I understand you've just received a bid from Simco."

"Which I'm turning down."

"Now, wait a minute. Don't just turn it down. The terms can be renegotiated." He moved confidently toward her. "If you think their offer isn't acceptable—"

"It's not that." She spoke quickly and stood up, instinctively positioning herself for defense. Only why should she be defensive? "I've simply decided not to do any more relocation tours."

"You what? What are you trying to do? Sabotage your business?"

"Of course not. I'm just doing what I originally intended. I plan to run my own business as I—"

"Right into bankruptcy!"

She stiffened. "I was doing very well without any assistance from you."

"Sure you were. Limping along with a broken-down bus, no insurance and no planning whatsoever. If I hadn't rammed Snowden down your throat, you'd have been flat on your face long before now."

She stared at him. *Rammed Snowden down your throat!* "Yes, that's exactly what you did, isn't it? You represented Snowden as someone desperately in need of help, when in reality he was no such thing!" *And I should have known better,* she thought, *seeing that beautiful well-equipped plant and all that up-front money.* Her fingers tensed on the prospectus and she looked down. Perhaps she'd known all along. But the planning, the working with Blake . . . She'd wanted to please him.

"Okay, okay." He shrugged slightly as if in resignation. "Perhaps I did misrepresent the facts a bit, but—"

"Misrepresent the facts! You manipulated me!" She couldn't help the surge of bitterness. She had fallen so easily under his spell.

"I transformed a failing tour company into a viable fast-growing concern with an excellent statewide reputation for its relocation tours. And I might add," he said, glaring down at her, "some small glimmer of financial stability."

"But," she said slowly, "that wasn't what I wanted." She hadn't quit her job to become a robot drawing up maps and delving into shopping centers.

"Oh?" He raised an eyebrow. "You joined New Ventures. I assumed you wanted our help in establishing a successful business."

"Success, yes. But in doing something I enjoy. Art seminars and—"

"Good Lord, Karin! We've been over this before. You've got to get over this art fetish. It isn't—"

"Stop it!" Her whole body prickled with the heat of anger. "You talk about art like it's something..." She faltered, searching for the right words. "Like it's putrid and degrading!"

"Not at all." He seemed confused by her vehemence. "I'm just saying there's no money in limiting yourself to art tours."

"There's more to life than money, Blake Connors."

"Granted, but—"

"I started doing art tours because that's what I like. And that's what I'm going to do. I may not become a millionaire, but I can make a living and enjoy it." She was not only angry now, but determined. She wouldn't be manipulated again.

"Be reasonable, Karin. Take advantage of our expertise. We have all the statistics and we know the risks, so we can calculate the best direction. We're a business incubator—"

"Yes, I know. You hatch big bright rich remarkably successful businesses, and I congratulate you. But," she said quietly, "I've just decided I don't want my business hatched."

"It's not time for you to make that decision." His face flushed with anger. "We have a contract. You haven't reached the graduation agreement yet."

"So, I'm a dropout." She brushed past him and started to open the door.

"Just a minute. This isn't a question of quitting. I've invested time and money in your project. You owe me—morally, ethically and contractually. And I mean to hold you to that contract."

"So, sue me!" Karin walked out, slamming the door behind her.

But as she went down the hall, her steps lagged as her brain finally caught up with her mouth. "So sue me" was intemperate and uncalled for, she admitted. Further, he *could* sue her. And win. She *did* owe him. He *had* invested time and money.

With a sinking heart she realized she was hoping he'd follow her. She quickened her steps. She resolved that she wouldn't allow him to chain her to the monotonous routine of relocation tours. Even if they were the biggest money-makers. He had no right.

He had a perfect right. She walked across the parking lot, seeing nothing but his face, his confident smile. Hearing nothing but his voice... "That's my job." He was proud of that job. He helped people. Like Snowden. "I was making these gourmet-cooking utensils in my garage and peddling them door-to-door before I hooked up with Blake," Snowden had told Karin. Like Keith Spencer. A warmth spread through Karin whenever she thought of that budding career. Dolly. She had pulled out before, as they put it, "reaching her full potential." But even so, she admitted that her stint with New Ventures had been beneficial.

And me, Karin reflected with a twinge of guilt. She had told Meg that by Christmas she'd be rolling in money. And she was, although it wasn't even Thanksgiving yet. She had a substantial bank account and no indebtedness, which made it easy to launch out on her own again. For all of that, she had to thank New Ventures. Still, did that mean they had the right to take over?

Anyway, Blake hadn't given Dolly a hard time when she left, Karin thought as she unlocked her car and positioned herself behind the wheel. "He was so understanding," Dolly had said, "especially when I told him that as a single mother with a teenage son I had other pressing responsibilities."

Sighing deeply, Karin started the car. *Okay, so I don't have that kind of responsibility! But I do have a right to run my business as I choose.* And she didn't choose to direct a national company with a big staff and mountains of research and paperwork. She, too, had rights, Mr. Blake Connors.

Sue her? Would it come to that? She hoped not. She didn't want to leave this way—in bitterness and anger.

She tried to think rationally. Wasn't there something in the contract about each company functioning as an independent unit? If she felt, and she did, that this was no longer possible, surely New Ventures would release her without rancor.

Anyway, she did have the right to leave. *And I'm glad I did. I'm glad to be free. Happy in my work and my life.*

Only she didn't feel happy. Or even very free. She felt alone, and a little lost.

IN THE CONFERENCE ROOM, Blake stood unmoving, the slam of the door reverberating in his brain.

Well, that was that. So be it.

He drew a deep breath, stuffed his hands into his pockets and walked to the window, shaking his head.

Damn! Damn! Damn! She couldn't see beyond her nose. Relocation of personnel, vital though it was, was just the beginning. She was on the threshold of a new and revolutionary approach to corporate transplantation. A business that would help break the tie that often occurred between competing cities trying to entice companies seeking a new location. She could work both sides, the companies looking for new ground, and the city, county or state in quest of new industry.

He turned and paced the room in exasperation, then was struck by a sudden thought. Had he fully explained everything he envisioned?

Well, damn it, he'd tried. No easy task. He'd had to demand, cajole...okay, manipulate her into allowing him to spend money and time, his own personal time, to develop the kind of expertise she would need. And now that she was succeeding, now that she'd gained a reputation as an expert in this relatively new field, now that the money was just beginning to roll in, she wanted out!

Absently he jingled his keys, remembering her comment—"I may not become a millionaire, but I can make a living and enjoy it."

Face it, Connors. She's tried to tell you. She has neither the inclination nor the ambition to develop the kind of business *you* envision.

She'd rather spend her time canning pineapples, hunting worms or lolling on some beach playing with her art!

Sue her? For being what she was? A chip off the old block—as dizzy as that aunt of hers.

He shrugged. You win some, you lose some. And he had more important tenants to consider. If he was going to make that trip to Monte Carlo with Holiday he'd better get a move on...

He pulled his hands out of his pockets and strode back to his office.

CHAPTER FOURTEEN

"'DECK THE HALLS with boughs of holly! Tra-la-la-la-la-la-la-la-la!'" sang the radio on his desk. "'Tis the season to be jolly! Tra-la-la—'"

Blake snapped it off. Glumly he contemplated the pile of papers before him. He was tired. It had been a grilling four weeks. Besides the tiresome trip to Monte Carlo, he had made three short trips to Philadelphia. After one of those trips, he flew to New York for Thanksgiving and took his parents out to dinner. Then four days in Memphis, where a friend wanted to join him in opening a New Ventures branch, followed by three days in Houston, where the city fathers were also urging him to open a branch. Tennessee, Texas or both? He could sure use the services of a relocation analyst. Karin Palmer. A lump rose in his throat as her image skittered through his mind. He swallowed the lump, willed the image to fade. No time to dwell on failures.

He picked up the prospectus from Blasco Tool. It looked good. The Wells Fargo financing had given it a big boost and they were expanding rapidly. Blake waited for that old surge of excitement when one of his tenants scored. It didn't come. He felt empty. He rubbed his eyes and looked down again, regarding the work before him with uncharacteristic distaste. Business! Abruptly he swung his chair around, turning his back to it.

The credenza behind his desk had been given over to Christmas cards and holiday decorations, carefully arranged by Vickie. The centerpiece was an oversize replica of an old-fashioned paperweight, its glass-enclosed dome containing a Christmas scene. Blake picked it up, wound the music box and shook it. Replacing it, he idly watched the snow fall on the little Santa Claus and his busy elves and listened to the tinkling "Jingle Bells."

He wondered why he felt so depressed. Christmas had never been a big deal to him, even when he was a child. Oh, sure, presents in the morning and dinner out at some fancy restaurant. Not like the excitement and bustle that went on at Pete's house. Blake sighed. He couldn't miss what he'd never had, could he?

And he was never alone Christmas Day. As usual, Pete would invite him to dinner. And he'd go. Pete and Thelma would radiate with warm hospitality, the children would climb on his knee, excited and grateful for whatever he brought them. And yet he always felt apart—an outsider they had taken pity on.

They always asked Vickie, too. But this year she was spending Christmas week at Tahoe with, of all people, Hank Lowell! Blake almost laughed out loud. Pete had been irate when Blake had assigned Lowell's Printing to Vickie. "You know she's against taking him on," Pete had said. "And didn't you see the sparks fly when they met?"

But something about the way the sparks flew had alerted Blake. Here was a man who could handle Vickie, he'd thought. And he'd been right.

His buzzer sounded and he flipped the switch. The receptionist's voice came over the intercom. "A Mrs. Dunlap is here and wishes to see you."

"Dunlap?" Who the hell was she?

"She said you'd remember her as Fran Powers."

Fran. He was transported back in time. Back to a shady college campus, a secluded nook in the park, back to his first bachelor apartment where he and Fran... Lord, how he had loved that woman! Fran. Fran Powers Dunlap. It had been ten years since he'd seen her—the night she'd told him she was marrying Ricky Dunlap. The pain of that last meeting was forgotten now, overshadowed by a thrill of anticipation. Fran!

"Mr. Connors?"

"Oh. Yes. Of course. Show her in." He switched off the intercom, rose and walked around his desk to greet her.

She was still beautiful. Tall, slender, just as he remembered. More polished, more sophisticated. Short mink jacket, beige knit dress, diamond stud earrings. The silver-blond hair no longer fell to her waist, but waved back from her face in a smart shoulder-length cut. The same slanting gray eyes, the same seductive smile and teasingly provocative manner. He found himself enveloped in a cloud of expensive perfume as she flung her arms around his neck and kissed him full on the lips.

He was still trying to get his bearings when she stepped back to survey him with admiring eyes. "Blake Connors. Handsome as ever."

He recovered his voice. "And you haven't changed a bit, except that you're even lovelier. It sure looks as if things are going well with you."

"I suppose you could say that. If breaking up a bad marriage is 'going well.'" Her lower lip pushed out in a little pout.

"Oh, Fran, I'm sorry."

"Don't be. The breakup was long past due. But let's not talk about that. I'll only be here a couple of days and we have a lot of catching up to do."

"Yes," he agreed, pulling out a chair for her. "What are you doing in this area?"

"I'm on my way to Palm Springs to spend Christmas with friends. But before I headed out, I called your mother to get your address. Couldn't come all this way without stopping to see you."

"Good," he said, wondering, Why now? After all these years. Where did she live, anyway? He thought it was somewhere in upstate New York.

"Your mother tells me you've become a regular ball of fire," Fran said, flashing him a bright smile. "Says your Philly plant covers ten blocks and that you own a big hunk of several extremely lucrative companies."

"Oh, Fran. You know how mothers are."

"Uh, huh. And I know how modest you are." Her eyes traveled over his tastefully furnished office, as if placing a price tag on each item. "But I want to hear all about how clever you are and how you've managed to accumulate all this..." She made a sweeping gesture reminiscent of something from the past. Something painful he couldn't quite put a finger on. "So, get your coat. You're going to take me to lunch and tell me how you've become such a big tycoon!"

He took her to the quiet Garden Room of the quaint Terrace Hotel. He took her there willingly, fully expecting to recapture some of the old magic. Expecting to relive the old feelings, when the wit and laughter of Fran Powers had so released him from the dull enclosure of his parents' scholarly flat.

The wit and laughter were still there, and she flattered him to the hilt. Amazingly she seemed to know about every big deal he'd pulled off in the past three years. He thought about that. She couldn't have gotten all that information from his mother, who never knew what his deals were. Fran rattled them off like a running tabulator—as if she'd carefully traced his progress.

"I read that great article about you in the *Economic Times*. You've gained quite a reputation for your unusual approach. You've succeeded in such a *variety* of businesses," she chortled.

"Oh, well..." He shrugged and took a sip of wine. Somehow her recounting didn't engender the old thrill of accomplishment.

"Of course, I always knew you had it in you," she said. "Oh, Blake, I'm so proud of you, of what you've done, starting with practically nothing."

Oddly he was reminded of another meal when another woman had said, "We've covered the rich-man-poor-man bit. Tell me about you. The real you."

He squirmed uncomfortably, wanting to change the drift of the conversation.

"Tell me about you," he said. "What have you been doing while I..." His voice trailed off, not finishing the *While I've been getting rich.*

She seemed eager to tell him. How the marriage had gone sour from the first. How she had tried. How the past five years had really been unbearable. How beastly Ricky was being about alimony, "and after I've given him the best years of my life!" And who was going to get the town house and the beach house and the different stocks and holdings too numerous for him to take in. But not for Fran. She must have a calculator for a brain, he thought.

He tried to appear interested, nodding sympathetically as he ate his salmon. But he was only half listening and was caught unawares when he realized she'd asked a direct question.

"Pardon?"

"So there's no Mrs. Connors, is there?" she repeated a little coyly. When he shook his head she went on, "No one special in your life?"

"No," he answered. *Yes,* he was thinking. *Someone who could be special if only...*

Fran reached across the table to touch his hand. "Perhaps what we had was too special, Blake. We were too young and foolish to know it and to hold on," she said with obviously feigned sadness. "But what we had was so great it spoiled any chance for either of us with anyone else."

He stared at her, shocked into silence. Realizing she was right. And realizing she was wrong—really wrong! At the time, he'd been so much in love with Fran, and it was only now, even as she spoke, that he could recognize it, define it as youthful infatuation. This visit, this repartee, was a come-on. Until now, he hadn't seen that.

Now she loomed vividly clear as a calculating, selfish and shallow woman. And to think, he mused, that ten years ago he was so shattered by her rejection, he'd refused to become emotionally involved with any other woman ever again.

Good Lord! Was he really that big a fool?

He felt relieved when he dropped Fran at her hotel. He was sorry, he told her, but pressing business prevented him from seeing her again before she left for Palm Springs.

He didn't go back to the office, but went instead to his condo. Still deep in thought, he felt peculiarly detached in the familiar living room. He glanced around. The room was immaculate, left in perfect order by the cleaning woman. Not even one Christmas ornament disrupted the elegant decor created by Wormsley and Weems, the most highly regarded decorators in the area. The powerful electronic gadgetry for audio and visual entertainment was excellently concealed, the heavy period furniture was masculine and comfortable, and the muted gray and burgundy tones of the furnishings were highlighted by carefully placed objets d'art.

Nothing seemed out of place—except the two pictures he had tacked above the marble fireplace right next to a finely detailed Japanese woodcut.

Blake stared at the caricature of himself. He had laughed when Keith gave it to him. In fact, he'd been very pleased. Now he felt sober and a little sad as, for the first time, he grasped its full significance. Was that what he was? A money machine, so concerned with industry and profits that all else was blotted from his mind?

Karin. His eyes focused on her watercolor of the ocean geyser bursting from the rocks, and suddenly he was back on a beach in Mendocino. He was sitting on a rock beside a woman who didn't seem to worry about material things, whose mind was full of big ideas about life and nature. A woman who took great pleasure in things you couldn't put a price on—chickens, vegetable gardens, her painting, the company of others. And, whether on a beach or standing beside a chicken coop, it was with this woman that he had experienced a tranquillity and happiness he had never known before.

And he'd refused to think of her except as a business! He had tried to change her into an entrepreneur as insensitive as Vickie or even, heaven forbid, a greedy opportunist like Fran.

Lord, he really was a fool!

"Oh, Meg, these turned out really well," said Karin, carefully lifting the lavishly decorated sugar cookies with a spatula.

Meg glanced over from the mincemeat pie she was edging. "They sure look good."

"Let me see. Delicious!" Bob announced as he crunched into a perfectly shaped star. "Hey, Karin, I haven't heard that phone ringing lately."

"I told you. I'm not scheduling any more trips till after New Year's. I intend to enjoy the holidays." In spite of the hollow ache in the pit of her stomach. Everything was just the same, she told herself as she breathed in the luscious odors of Christmas baking.

"If you ask me, you made a mistake leaving New Ventures." Bob leaned against the counter and reached over to sample a brownie. "That guy's got a head on his shoulders."

Karin swallowed, wishing he wouldn't mention "that guy."

"She's not asking you," Meg said. "And I wish you'd stop mooching and bring in the tree so Karin can decorate it."

"Don't see why you had such a big one sent to us," grumbled Bob. "That stand's too little for it."

"There's a bigger stand on the second shelf in the garage. And bring in that box of decorations next to it." Meg bent over to place the pie in the oven just as the doorbell rang. "Get that, would you, Karin? It'll be Lisa Turner with the pecans."

It wasn't Lisa. It was Blake. Karin's heart turned over, and her mind was in such a tumult she couldn't move. Puzzlement—why was he here? Joy—did it matter? Dismay—she looked a fright and he was taking it all in. She knew that look of amused assessment.

He confirmed it. "You have flour on your nose."

Her hand flew up to brush it off. But there was nothing she could do about the cookie dough on her T-shirt, her disheveled hair, her—

"Aren't you going to ask me in?"

"Oh. Yes, of course," she stammered, stepping back.

"Thanks." He closed the door behind him. "I wouldn't blame you if you didn't. I was pretty hard on you, wasn't I?"

It came back to her then. The harsh words. The anger. She'd forgotten all of that, lost in the void his absence made in her life.

"It was just that...it...well, we just had different opinions." Had he come to ask her to change her mind? Would she?

"Bring in the pecans," Meg called from the kitchen. "I'm all ready."

"It's not Lisa," Karin called back. "It's Blake."

"Sorry. No pecans," Blake said, smiling.

"Oh, don't be silly." Meg came out, wiping her hands on her apron. "It's just that Lisa was shelling the nuts and I was going to show her how to sugarcoat them and..." She shrugged. "How nice to see you, Mr. Connors. Do come on back and—"

"Help me with this damn tree," Bob panted as he dragged it from the patio. "Don't know why these women pick the biggest one on the lot."

Karin watched Blake remove his coat and go over to take a firm hold on the pine while Bob tried to fit it into the stand. He seemed completely absorbed, as he was with anything he did. How many times had she watched him intently discussing some problem with Pete or Vickie. While she stood apart.

She resented his being here. She'd been getting on with her life, making her own plans. She had stopped thinking about him . . . well, almost. *And he just walks in, upsetting everything!*

"Better get that other batch of cookies ready, Karin. The pies will be out soon," Meg said, breaking into her thoughts.

Karin was glad to escape to the kitchen. She tried to compose herself as she moved about, automatically rolling out the dough, cutting it into various shapes and decorating each. There was no reason to be disturbed by Blake's presence. She had made her decision and she had no intention of returning to New Ventures. But she was attuned to every movement in the family room as the two men, between cursing and laughing and under the constant direction of Meg, struggled to get the tree upright.

"No, it still tilts a little to the left," Meg was saying. "There. That's fine. It's fine, Bob! Don't touch it. There now, Mr. Connors. You've done a good job."

"Hey, what about me?" Bob exclaimed. "If I hadn't—"

"All right, both of you have done a good job," Meg said, laughing. "And you'll both be rewarded. How does oyster stew followed by hot mincemeat pie sound?"

"Sounds great," said Bob.

"Good." Meg nodded. "Then as soon as you string the lights and—"

"Hey, that's Karin's job," Bob insisted. "We're not fooling with all that stuff."

"Speak for yourself," said Blake. "Where are the lights? If that pie tastes as good as it smells . . ."

In the kitchen Karin heard his familiar chuckle and was appalled when her heart gave a little lurch. *Oh, don't,* she warned herself. *Don't be taken in by him again.* His chuckle, his smile, that way he had of quirking his eyebrow... She had to remember to forget.

The cookies were out of the oven, sixteen-year-old Lisa had arrived with the pecans, and Meg shooed Karin out of the kitchen. No more avoiding Blake. But, thank goodness, they weren't alone. They could hear Meg and Lisa chatting in the nearby kitchen, and there was Bob across the room in his big chair by the fire, buried in his newspaper. Their presence lessened the constraint Karin felt, and she was able to laugh and talk quite naturally with Blake as they strung the lights.

"Fill the stand with ginger ale instead of water," Meg called from the kitchen. "The sugar keeps the tree green and fresh. Don't you love that pine scent? It always says Christmas to me."

"I thought she had a thing against sugar," Blake whispered to Karin.

"Anything goes at Christmas." Karin dimpled. "We could never feed the crowd we have on fruit and nuts."

"You always have a crowd?"

"Oh, yes. The Turners have us over on Thanksgiving and we have them for Christmas dinner, and there are six of them counting the in-laws. And this year, Dolly and Keith are coming, too." She hesitated. "We'd love to have you join us if you don't have other plans," she added, keeping her voice casual.

"I was hoping you'd ask. Thank you."

She bent her head to hide a flush of pleasure and began to delve into the box of ornaments. He must have had dozens of invitations, but he would be here! Suddenly she was glad he'd stopped by and she didn't care why he'd come. They were sitting on the floor sorting out decorations, and she lifted out one of the crude little bells fashioned from the tops of old frozen orange-juice containers. "We made these one year when I was a Brownie," she said, swinging it by the cord and remembering how carefully she had painted hers.

"That's pretty clever." He was looking not at the ornament but at her, and there was something in his expression... "I can see you as a Brownie, busy having fun. And I can tell at a glance that this is your handiwork." He picked up the bell to examine it closely.

"Oh, but you're wrong!" She burst into a laugh. "That's not even mine. That's Carol Jamison's. She said hers was crooked. See there, where it's bent a little?" Karin pointed. "And she was planning to take it to her dad who was in the hospital, so I exchanged mine with hers."

"Yes," he said quietly, "that's the kind of thing you'd do."

"Well, she was crying and upsetting everybody, so to shut her up I—" She broke off because he was looking at her in a way that made her heart turn over.

He shook his head. "No. It was because you are you. Some people just have the tinsel and glitter of Christmas, but you have the real spirit."

"Oh, my. Such compliments from Mr. Santa Claus himself."

He frowned. "Me?"

She nodded. It was fun to tease him. "You. Just as I said when you sent me that four-thousand-dollar check!" She shook her head. "Honestly, I'd never heard of such a thing!"

He smiled. "Oh, that."

"Yes, that. And don't discount it." She balanced on her knees to wag a finger at him. "Tell me. What would you have done if I had kept it?"

"Well, er, I don't know. I suppose I—"

"I'll tell you. You would calmly have set about telling me how to use it to make more money."

"Maybe," he said, grinning. "For a percentage of the profits."

"No reason you shouldn't practice what you preach. You do a darn good job and you deserve the rewards." She gave his shoulder a little shake. "But that's not to say you only care about money."

"The way Keith sees it, I do. You should see the caricature he did of me."

"I know. He told me about it."

He grimaced. "A greedy dictatorial money-grubber with a Midas touch."

"Don't you dare say that." She put a finger over his mouth. "That's not what Keith meant, and you know it. You should hear him talk about you. He's so proud of you, and so grateful for what you did for him—the way you do for almost anyone who needs it—"

"Karin, dear sweet Karin." He kissed the tip of each finger, then held the palm of her hand against his cheek. "You are so kind."

"I'm not being kind! There's not a greedy selfish bone in your entire body. And New Ventures? Why, it's like being part of a family, a strong supportive family. I've been there, remember? I've talked to people and I know your operation helps."

"You really mean that, don't you?"

"Yes, I do."

"Then you'll rejoin us?"

She drew her hand away and sank back on her heels, feeling bereft and a little foolish. As usual she'd been carried away by the man himself. She'd been concerned and trying to reassure him. As if he needed it! He was confident, competent and always able to zero in on exactly what he wanted. But somehow, for just a moment, she had thought he'd missed her as much as she'd missed him. Stupid! Stupid! He was all business and she knew it. *She* wasn't the real attraction. Well, he wouldn't get her back doing those relocation tours!

"Now wait. Don't look like that. Just listen a minute," he said. "You worked hard. And you built up a great reputation."

"Yes, so I did." She had done it to please him. But it hadn't been what *she* wanted. She straightened. She would not be manipulated again.

"A reputation is a valuable commodity," he went on calmly. "It would be a shame to throw it away. And in this relatively new field the potentials are endless."

She was silent, watching his eyes light up with the old fire as the innovative ideas took shape. How could she dampen his enthusiasm? He *was* a dollars-and-cents man—that was part of him—and didn't she love him for that, as well? She felt her resolve slipping.

"I had a great idea the other day," he said. "This kid came into my office. Not really a kid, I guess. She's twenty-one. Anyway, she and her grandfather started this sight-seeing tour company, mostly of the gold country. He's a retired forest ranger and knows the area." He shook his head. "A seasonal venture at best, and I don't know why they couldn't see that."

Because they didn't have you to point it out, she thought, amused in spite of herself.

"Anyway," he continued, "they ran into big trouble. Her grandmother became ill and the old man has to stay home with her. This kid has been trying to struggle along on her own. She's really industrious and quite personable. Karin, listen," he said, taking both her hands in his and speaking earnestly and persuasively.

Karin listened. Here was vintage Blake Connors, seeing another's need, planning, helping, finding a solution. And it was a great solution. A partnership with someone who could do the relocation while she continued with the art tours.

"All right," she agreed. "I'll do it."

"Great! We'll get started right after the holidays. But I'll let her know about the plan tomorrow. I'm sure she'll be pleased and relieved." He chuckled. "It'll be like giving her a present. After all, it is Christmas."

"Don't see why that should signify," Karin said, her dimples dancing.

"What do you mean?"

"I mean it wasn't Christmas when you dumped that check on me. And it wasn't Christmas when you spent all that advertising money on Keith's caricatures. And don't tell me you didn't, because I know *he* didn't have the money. And it wasn't Christmas when you pulled that Mendocino bed-and-breakfast place out of the—"

"Okay, okay. Enough." Blake looked embarrassed. "Now, let's get down to business. Of course you'll have to train this kid. The Simco project is still available. If you pick it up you'll have to..."

But this time his enthusiasm didn't catch her imagination. The more he talked, the more she felt trapped, buried in maps, brochures and training sessions. This was the time she had meant to plan and schedule the art tours. But once again, she'd be doing what he wanted instead.

"You're shameless!" She was almost angry. "You came over here on purpose to inveigle me into doing something I don't want to!"

"No, you're wrong. I didn't—"

"Oh, yes, you did. You did it again, didn't you? Manipulated me..." She broke off, hurt because today's visit wasn't what she'd thought, what she'd hoped for... "It's always business with you, isn't it?"

"That's not true. Not exactly, anyway. I only thought... Oh, hell! What did I say to set you off?" He ran a hand through his hair. "Look, I thought if we talked things out you could see the best thing to do."

"Sure you did. You know what you are, Blake Connors? You're a con man!"

"Now wait a minute." He reached out a hand, which she ignored.

"And you came here on purpose to con me into doing what you wanted." She stood up, feeling the tears sting her eyelids. She had to get away before she made a fool of herself.

He stood quickly and grabbed her arm. "No. You're wrong, Karin. I came to ask you—"

"And you succeeded, didn't you?" She tried to pull away. "You wanted me to rejoin your firm and do those relocation tours!"

"Damn it!" He sounded angry now. "I don't care if you never rejoin New Ventures and never do another relocation tour. I didn't come for that. I came here to ask you to marry me!"

It would be so painful working with him when what she wanted was— Her head jerked up. "What? What did you say?"

"I said I don't care if you never do another—"

"*No.* The other. You said you came here to ask me..." Her voice faltered. Maybe she hadn't heard right. Maybe it was all in her head.

"I said I came here to ask you to marry me. I was waiting until... Oh, damn it. This isn't the time or the place, and now you're mad."

"No, I'm not mad." Just dizzy. As if she was on a roller coaster and couldn't get off. First up, then down. Did he mean it?

"Oh, Karin," he said, taking her by the shoulders and looking down at her. "I've been such a fool, trying to change you when you're exactly what I want. I promise you can paint, raise chickens or whatever. And you needn't bother with the relocation tours. Karin, I love you. If you'll marry me, I promise—"

"Oh, Blake!" She flung herself into his arms, bursting with happiness. He meant it! He really loved her!

"Yes, yes, I'll marry you. Oh, I love you so much, relocation tours and all."

"And I love you," he whispered in her ear, holding her as if he'd never let her go. "I've been so miserable. Everything, even the business, has gone sour for me. I thought it was the season. You know—the holiday blues you get when you're alone. I really had 'em bad."

"Me, too," she murmured, her voice muffled against his chest. And she hadn't even been alone.

"But it wasn't the holidays. When you opened that door and I saw you standing there with flour on your nose, everything fell into place. It was like I'd come home. It was *you* I was missing—you, with your happy loving always-Christmas spirit."

Always Christmas. That's how it would be every day, Karin thought, as long as Blake was with her. She wrapped her arms around him, drinking in his kiss, feeling the ecstasy flow through her like wine, intoxicating her with love and joy and peace.

And somewhere in the distance the sound of clapping.

"Why the applause, Bob Palmer?" came Meg's voice. "We've finished the pecans and the stew's ready and

nothing's happened. They haven't hung a single ornament."

"You're wrong there, my pet!" Bob's hearty laugh
rang out. "Everything's happened. The only thing missing is the mistletoe!"

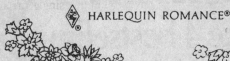

Take 4 bestselling love stories FREE

Plus get a FREE surprise gift!

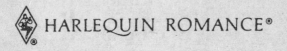

HARLEQUIN ROMANCE®

Norah Bloomfield's father is recovering from his heart attack, and her sisters are getting married. So Norah's feeling a bit unneeded these days, a bit left out....

Orchard Valley

And then a cantankerous "cowboy" called Rowdy Cassidy crashes into her life!

"The Orchard Valley trilogy features three delightful, spirited sisters and a trio of equally fascinating men. The stories are rich with the romance, warmth of heart and humor readers expect, and invariably receive, from Debbie Macomber."

—Linda Lael Miller

Don't miss the Orchard Valley trilogy by Debbie Macomber:

VALERIE   Harlequin Romance #3232 (November 1992)
STEPHANIE   Harlequin Romance #3239 (December 1992)
NORAH   Harlequin Romance #3244 (January 1993)

Look for the special cover flash on each book!

Available wherever Harlequin books are sold.   ORC-3

HARLEQUIN HISTORICAL
CHRISTMAS
STORIES · 1992 ·

Capture the magic and romance of Christmas in the 1800s with HARLEQUIN HISTORICAL CHRISTMAS STORIES 1992, a collection of three stories by celebrated historical authors. The perfect Christmas gift!

Don't miss these heartwarming stories, available in November wherever Harlequin books are sold:

MISS MONTRACHET REQUESTS by Maura Seger
CHRISTMAS BOUNTY by Erin Yorke
A PROMISE KEPT by Bronwyn Williams

Plus, as an added bonus, you can receive a FREE keepsake Christmas ornament. Just collect four proofs of purchase from any November or December 1992 Harlequin or Silhouette series novels, or from any Harlequin or Silhouette Christmas collection, and receive a beautiful dated brass Christmas candle ornament.

Mail this certificate along with four (4) proof-of-purchase coupons plus $1.50 postage and handling (check or money order—do not send cash), payable to Harlequin Books, to: **In the U.S.:** P.O. Box 9057, Buffalo, NY 14269-9057; **In Canada:** P.O. Box 622, Fort Erie, Ontario, L2A 5X3.

ONE PROOF OF PURCHASE	Name: _____
	_____
	Address: _____
	_____
	City: _____
	State/Province: _____
	Zip/Postal Code: _____

HX92POP   093 KAG

"Sunday night," Jane said, suddenly eager to end the call. "Here's my taxi, gotta run."

"Okay. Well…be careful."

Jane said goodbye and disconnected the call, wondering if her friend's reaction was out of concern, or the fact that Jane had done something so out of character?

She climbed into the taxi with her overnight bag and tamped down a spike of apprehension. Maybe she *was* getting in over her head.

Her nervousness mounted during the taxi ride to her hotel, as she got a close-up view of the soaring casinos and clubs, their neon signs and lights impressive even in broad daylight—she couldn't imagine how frantic the atmosphere would be at night.

As for the Bellagio hotel itself, the fountains alone took her breath away, with series of columns of water spraying into the sky, then falling like rows of dancers, only to rise again in another brilliant explosion.

Even the water in Vegas had pizzazz.

Walking into the hotel lobby, she felt like an awestruck schoolgirl. The centerpiece was an in-

credible Dale Chihuly glass sculpture, a riotou plosion of fused and intertwined flowers and so delicate in appearance that they defie material they were made from. The piece was binding, more beautiful even than the Cl pieces she'd seen on display in the Atlanta B cal Gardens. At the time she wondered that ind als could afford to own a Chihuly piece priv

And now, Jane realized suddenly, *she* The notion was still mind-boggling.

In addition to the sculpture, the lobby fea conservatory and garden, soaring ceilings an that seemed to extend forever. She felt small of place in her casual clothes, holding her tir night bag. Everyone around her looke money—women wore designer dresses a heels, men wore sport coats and western boo pensive dress shoes. Self-consciously, she up to the front desk to check in, but the pret haired desk clerk smiled warmly, putting he

"Welcome to Las Vegas," the woman sa you here on vacation?"

Jane nodded. "The reservation is unde

The clerk gave her directions, then took Jane's suitcase for safekeeping.

Jane followed the directions to the salon, but when she got to the entrance, she hesitated. Then, as if the powers that be knew she needed a push, the doors slid open on their own. She walked in tentatively, wondering why she had such a difficult time succumbing to the ministrations that she applied to others on a daily basis. Was it because she feared the outcome would be less than favorable, *and* that her appearance couldn't be improved upon?

A beautiful blonde wearing an aqua-colored lab coat walked up to her. "How can we help you today?"

Jane sighed. "Can you make me look like you?"

The woman smiled, angled her head, and put her finger under Jane's chin. "I'll do even better— I'll make you look like *you*."

Flashing back to her encounter with Bette Valentine, Jane wondered how other people could look at her and see something that she herself couldn't see.

As she followed the woman to a workstation, Jane desperately hoped that her inner wild child was marginally more attractive.

PERRY COULDN'T get a flight to Vegas until noon. He fretted in his cramped seat in coach for the entire trip knowing that Jane had a half-day head start on him. A naive tourist could get into a lot of trouble in Vegas in a very short time. And a naive tourist intent on finding trouble…he didn't even want to think about it.

When he landed, he phoned Theresa as he strode through the airport. "Did you find her?"

"She's registered at the Bellagio. I booked you a room." Her voice rang with disapproval.

"Thanks. And don't judge me."

"You're chasing a woman you barely know across the country right after she won the lottery— what am I supposed to think?"

"It's not the way it looks. Besides, you were the one who insisted that I take a vacation."

"Just do the right thing."

"Goodbye." Perry frowned and disconnected the phone call, then joined the taxi line. He hadn't been to Vegas in ages, but it didn't take long to fall under the influence of the energy in the air and become acclimated to the increased pace. His adrenaline